Off Off Broadway Festival Plays
6th Series

Selected by New York theatre critics and the editorial
staff of Samuel French, Inc., as the most important plays in the
Sixth Annual Off-Off Broadway Original Short Play Festival
sponsored by Double Image Theatre, Inc.

SEDUCTION DUET
by M. H. Appleman

A BENCH AT THE EDGE
by Luigi Jannuzzi

PERIOD
by Richard McBrien

A SAMUEL FRENCH ACTING EDITION

SAMUEL FRENCH
FOUNDED 1830

SAMUELFRENCH.COM
SAMUELFRENCH-LONDON.CO.UK

Seduction Duet

for my mother, and for Phil

SEDUCTION DUET was first presented at the Circle Repertory Theater on May 14, 1980. Director, John Bard Manulis. Lighting, Denise Yaney. Costumes, Joan E. Weiss. Stage Manager, Alice Galloway. It was subsequently presented in the Sixth Annual Off-Off Broadway Short Play Festival, at St. Clement's Theatre, on May 28, 1981, under the aegis of the Circle Repertory Company. Director, John Bard Manulis. Lighting, Gordon A. Juel. Stage Manager, Rob Meiksins.

CAST

CYNTHIA . . . . *Toni James*
MATT . . . . *Jeff Daniels, original production*
Danton Stone, second production

CAST OF CHARACTERS:

CYNTHIA — young and appealing, with a ready laugh and
  sense of humor that help to conceal her underlying
  shyness and seriousness. She is wearing an attractive outfit — a dressy blouse and full skirt.
MATT — young, likable, and thoughtful, he tries to ap-
  pear casual and self-confident, in order to disguise
  his feelings of insecurity. He is well dressed, in a
  subdued suit, shirt, and tie.

Seduction Duet

TIME: *the present. Late Friday night.*

SETTING: *the living room of* Cynthia's *tastefully decorated apartment. Included in the furnishings are a full-size sofa, at center, with a Mexican serape, as a throw, over the back of it, and on it, several small sofa pillows and a toy stuffed whale, two feet long; easy chairs to each side of the sofa; a coffee table in front of it, on which are a few books and magazines, including one on conservation and one on butterflies, and a figurine of a dolphin; nearby are two lamps. There are also a stereo set, a cabinet containing drinking glasses and cocktail napkins, and some bookcases filled with books. Hanging on a wall are a large framed print or photograph of a monarch butterfly, and a mirror. As a seating area, down center left, are several large floor pillows. There are two doorways.*

AT RISE: *the stage is dark. From offstage, outside the front door, footsteps are heard, and indistinct talk. The door opens.* CYNTHIA *enters, switches on a light, turns to* MATT, *who remains offstage, outside the door. They both are ill at ease.*

CYNTHIA. (*At the door, just inside; with a hesitant smile.*) It was nice of you to bring me home.

MATT. (*Still offstage; sounding uncertain.*) My pleasure . . . So then . . . See you Monday.

CYNTHIA. Thanks again for rescuing me. I'm still shaking.

MATT. Would you like me to stay a while? Until you recover? (MATT *enters, nervous.*)

CYNTHIA. Oh, I think I've recovered. (*She laughs, embarrassed.*)

MATT. Well, OK. (*He starts to leave, stops, turns back to* CYNTHIA.) But didn't you just say you were still shaking?

CYNTHIA. Yes, I did! Why don't you come in and stay a while? (*She quickly slams the door.*)

MATT. (*Jumping, startled by the slamming door.*) OH! . . . K!

CYNTHIA. And—and talk! (*Laughing, flustered, she turns on more lights.*)

MATT. Sure! After all, it's early yet.

CYNTHIA. It's twelve-thirty.

MATT. Early in the morning! (*A grin.*) Early in the week, too. (*He laughs.*)

CYNTHIA. (*Laughing with him.*) Oh! Yes! It's tomorrow already. (*Their laughter fades into awkward smiles, and a pause.*) I can tell you this—it's the last office party I go to. If you hadn't . . .

MATT. Just in time.

CYNTHIA. I'll say—just in time. He was ready to rape me.

MATT. Rape! I don't know if you'd call it—that.

CYNTHIA. Rape is rape, whatever you call it. (*She double-locks the door.*) A woman can sense these things, you know—long before they happen. (*A shudder.*) Ohh. I'm getting the shakes again. (*A sideways glance at him.*) I'd rather change the subject, if it's all the same to you.

MATT. (*Uncomfortable.*) Good idea! I like your place.

CYNTHIA. Thanks. Did you notice that after you ran in and saved me, he tried to laugh it off? (*She rearranges the sofa pillows.*)

MATT. Big. That is, for somebody who lives — all alone. (*An uneasy laugh.*)

CYNTHIA. What kind of a monster would laugh at rape? But let's not talk about it any more. (*She punches a pillow, to fluff it up.*)

MATT. (*Sobering abruptly; businesslike.*) Right. How do you like working at Frick and Frick?

CYNTHIA. Imagine, laughing at rape! Just like a man. (*Hastily.*) I mean a man like that. And did you see how he tried to wiggle out of it? (*She vigorously shakes out the serape.*)

MATT. Is it hard to get into your field? Computers, that is!

CYNTHIA. He said it was nothing. Nothing! Can you believe calling rape nothing? But let's get our minds on something else, OK? (*She briskly refolds the serape, carefully replaces it on the back of the sofa, and puts the toy stuffed whale near it.*)

MATT. That's fine with me, Cynthia! May I call you — Cyn?

CYNTHIA. As long as it doesn't give you any ideas.

MATT. Ideas? . . . Oh! No! (*An embarrassed laugh.*) I never even thought of . . . (*Quickly.*) Not that you're not attractive! Because you are. Very. (*A shy smile.*) You light up the whole — office.

CYNTHIA. (*Upset.*) That's what *he* said, just before he . . . (*She stops.*)

MATT. (*Taken aback.*) Harold? He did?

CYNTHIA. Everybody was partying down the hall, and he . . . Is he a friend of yours?

MATT. Well, yes . . . No! I mean . . . We both joined the accounting department about the same time. I can't help that, can I? (*Laughing uneasily, speaking faster.*) We take the same coffee breaks, and we brown-bag together every day. But I hardly know him! (*Rattled.*) What I mean is—not very well. We have nothing in common. Except our corned beef sandwiches. But he likes pumpernickel and I prefer rye with horseradish mustard, and . . .

CYNTHIA. (*Cutting in; aghast.*) You have to eat with him?

MATT. (*Thrown into confusion.*) He takes his coffee with double cream and sugar! And I like mine . . . Well, my desk happens to be right next to his desk. But that doesn't mean . . .

CYNTHIA. (*Horrified.*) His desk! Oh! It was awful! On top of his desk! On all those pencils! (*Looking at him, wide-eyed.*) Matt, I tried to get away, but he's . . . He's an animal! And then . . . (*Ecstatic.*) There you were! Rushing in to face an unknown danger! You! You! So brave! So strong! . . . Ohh, it makes me faint to think of it . . . I suppose I sound like a helpless idiot.

MATT. (*Flattered; trying to be modest.*) No, you don't. Anybody'd be upset about that. I'm just glad I heard you scream. If I hadn't run in . . . Well, just think what *else* might have happened.

CYNTHIA. (*Gasping.*) Ohh!

MATT. No! Don't think about it!

CYNTHIA. He tricked me! He said he wanted to show me something on his desk. (*Appalled.*) Of course I had no idea he meant *that* thing.

MATT. (*Shocked.*) WHAT!

CYNTHIA. Yes!

MATT. HAROLD?

CYNTHIA. Buckmaster.

MATT. He couldn't have! He said he'd take it easy!

CYNTHIA. What? When?

MATT. (*Flustered.*) When — what?

CYNTHIA. When did he say that?

MATT. When — when you were yelling! And — and — and I ran in! And I dragged him away from you! Don't you remember? *Take it easy*, he said.

CYNTHIA. Everything went black for a minute.

MATT. Thank god.

CYNTHIA. What? Why?

MATT. Why don't you try to relax?

CYNTHIA. (*Agitated.*) That's exactly what *he* said! Oh, why can't I stop thinking about it!

MATT. Maybe you should lie down. (CYNTHIA *gasps, looks at* MATT. MATT *looks at* CYNTHIA, *dismayed.*) He said that, too.

CYNTHIA. (*Starting to do an exercise, rolling her head around slowly.*) Could you excuse me a second? (CYNTHIA *moves away from* MATT *to do more exercises, shaking her body loose, bending to touch her toes.*) I'm all choked up, even now . . . This helps, sometimes. (*Facing front, she squats, frog-like, hands on floor, and moves her arms in and out between her knees, as she bounces up and down.*)

MATT. (*After watching her for a few moments.*) Mind if I join you? (*Moving to* CYNTHIA'S *side,* MATT *begins to do the same frog-like exercise; also facing front.* CYNTHIA *smiles, continuing the exercise.* MATT *smiles, enjoying it.*) It does help.

CYNTHIA. (*Breathing hard from the exertion.*) Some women can take an assault like that, right in stride. But I just can't. You must think I'm a little bit crazy.

MATT. (*Still exercising; panting.*) Not at all. As a matter of fact, I admire you for it. It's a very rare quality these days.

CYNTHIA. Insanity? (*She laughs, gets down on the floor to do sit-ups.*)

MATT. (*Taking off his jacket, loosening his tie.*) There's a revolution going on, you know. All around us. (*He gets a sofa pillow, throws it on the floor.*) It's already spread into the high schools. Junior highs, too. (MATT *stands on his head on the pillow, legs splayed awkwardly.* CYNTHIA *watches him, impressed, goes on exercising.*) Everybody's doing it. Younger and younger. Even fourth-graders.

CYNTHIA. Fourth-graders! Are you sure?

MATT. (*Still standing on his head.*) Nine-year-old nymphets and Little League studs—running loose on every playground in America. You're shocked by it, aren't you?

CYNTHIA. (*Panting; still doing sit-ups.*) Well, I don't know . . .

MATT. Great! It's terrific to find a woman who can still be shocked by sex.

CYNTHIA. Oh! I am, I am!

MATT. Just like the girl that married dear old dad—you know what I mean?

CYNTHIA. Yes, yes! Everyone's always telling me I look just like my mother.

MATT. That's wonderful.

CYNTHIA. (*Moving on her knees, to speak directly to his upside-down head.*) It's so refreshing to hear you talk. I haven't heard a man say that word for years.

MATT. Wonderful?

CYNTHIA. Married.

MATT. (*Falling over with a crash from his head-stand.*) I said THAT?

CYNTHIA. (*Singing brightly to him; smiling.*) "I want a girl just like the girl that married dear old dad . . ."

MATT. Oh! Yes . . .

CYNTHIA. (*Continuing to sing with zest.*) "She was a pearl, and the only girl that dad-dy ever had. A good old-fashioned girl with heart so true . . ."

MATT. (*Cutting in.*) Amazing! You even know the tune. You're one in a billion, you know it? (*Still on the floor, he lies on his side and does leg-raises.*) Most women these days just open up, and let 'er roll.

CYNTHIA. They do? My god! I mean, my goodness.

MATT. Without the slightest hesitation.

CYNTHIA. You seem to know all about it.

MATT. Well, I guess I might as well tell you. I may be an accountant by day. But my secret passion is—reading.

CYNTHIA. What a coincidence—I love to read!

MATT. I read everything about sex I can get my hands on. (*Hastily.*) I mean about the sexual revolution. Sociology, demography, anthropology, physiology . . .

CYNTHIA. So do I! Psychology, endocrinology—novels . . . (CYNTHIA *begins to do side-straddle hops.*)

MATT. (*Watching* CYNTHIA; *still doing leg-raises.*) Like, for instance—I can't resist the demographic curve. It's our worst problem—at the root of all the others.

CYNTHIA. You think so?

MATT. Put sex and demography together, and what do you get? (*He looks at* CYNTHIA, *expectant, one leg suspended in the air.* CYNTHIA *stops exercising, ponders a moment, perplexed.*) Overpopulation. (*He gets to his feet.*)

CYNTHIA. Oh! Yes! I've been reading about that, too. (*She again does side-straddle hops.*)

MATT. (*Warming into a prepared speech; starting to run in place.*) Right this minute, there are four and a half billion people on earth. But do you know how many more new persons will be added to the world in just one week? (CYNTHIA *shakes her head, wide-eyed.*) Over one and a half million!

CYNTHIA. How do you keep those big numbers in your head?

MATT. (*Continuing to run in place; panting.*) Well, I'm an accountant, remember. By this time next year, the world will have over eighty-four million *more* mouths to feed.

CYNTHIA. So altogether that'd make . . . Whew! That's a lot of breakfasts!

MATT. A total of four billion, five hundred eighty-four million, three hundred thousand, and . . .

CYNTHIA. And lunches, and dinners, and snacks. Where will it all come from?

MATT. Who knows? (*Somber.*) Famine, starvation . . .

CYNTHIA. Hey, are you hungry? (*She starts to jog her way to the kitchen, then stops when* MATT *demurs.*)

MATT. I stuffed myself at the party. So the world will double in only thirty-five years—if not sooner. That's nine billion people.

CYNTHIA. Nine billion people! By the .time I'm . . . Never mind. (*She crosses to the mirror, adjusts her clothes, fixes her hair.*)

MATT. You see, in past epochs there was a balance—because of the plague, and the pox, and so forth. But now, with the marvels of modern medicine, sex has led to a—a silent explosion—heard round the world! (*He stops running in place, tucks in his shirt, straightens his tie, puts his jacket back on.*)

CYNTHIA. The people explosion.

MATT. Unrestrained, uncontrolled . . .

CYNTHIA. And so fast! Twice as many people, in only thirty-five years! It's scary.

MATT. Geometric progression.

CYNTHIA. But we could do something about it, couldn't we? If everybody would just keep in mind one small number—such an appealing little number, too.

MATT. Two?

CYNTHIA. Right! Two! . . . Kids.

MATT. If only it were possible. Just think, maybe then we could solve some of our other problems—hunger, water shortages, pollution, toxic waste . . .

CYNTHIA. It's the only answer. Two, and no more. Maybe less. What do you think, Matt?

MATT. Well, I . . . (*Doubletake.*) I'm being hypothetical!

CYNTHIA. How do you feel about adoption?

MATT. Adoption! I'm talking about the demographic curve, flattening out.

CYNTHIA. So am I. Isn't it funny how such an enormous problem—a global disaster—turns out to be so individual, and so—private. To think that two people, and how they—do it . . . Well, it's no wonder that some people think they shouldn't do it at all.

MATT. On the other hand, Cynthia—recent physiological studies show that too much *not* doing it is very bad—for the body.

CYNTHIA. Bad for the mind, too. *Mens sana in corpore sano*, right?

MATT. Right. That's why the word "puritanical" has all those ugly connotations. Too much Anglo-Saxon repression.

CYNTHIA. Sexual repression has always been very Protestant.

MATT. And very Catholic.

CYNTHIA. And Jewish.

MATT. Don't forget the Muslims.

CYNTHIA. How could I? Of course, repression isn't good for anybody. But it always seems to be worse for women—like everything else. That is, it was. *Now*—as you point out—the sexual revolution is on. And the terrible thing is—as you point out—it's just as bad!

MATT. Well, I don't know if . . .

CYNTHIA. (*Going on urgently.*) If we just wouldn't go to such extremes! Do you realize—the continuous rise in rape is still rising? Not to mention incest—which is setting record highs. I was reading about incest just last night—in "Family Circle" . . . And on top of all that—the infections—the diseases! V.D. is everywhere!

MATT. It was on TV this morning . . . While I was eating breakfast.

CYNTHIA. I'm almost afraid to leave my apartment sometimes, after watching the news on TV. It's those health tips that get me. S.T.D., that's all they talk about. (MATT *looks puzzled.*) Sexually transmitted diseases. (*She turns away, flustered.*)

MATT. (*Looking uncomfortable; putting a sofa pillow on his lap.*) You're even taking a chance going to the movies these days.

CYNTHIA. And how about the swinging discos?

MATT. And the singles bars!

CYNTHIA. Oh, I'm not into the bar thing at all!

MATT. I'm not, either. And I'm definitely not into the massage thing.

CYNTHIA. (*An embarrassed laugh.*) Never! I'm into— uhh—mutual interests!

MATT. Backgammon?

CYNTHIA. I'd like to learn.

MATT. How about tennis?

CYNTHIA. And sailing!

MATT. And skiing!

CYNTHIA. And Chinese!

MATT. And scintillating conversation! In any language!

CYNTHIA. Yes! I'm especially heavy into conversation. In English. (*A smile.*) Like this. Finding out what a person's really like, you know what I mean?

MATT. I know just what you mean — feeling a person out.

CYNTHIA. (*Suspicious.*) Just what do you mean?

MATT. I mean, I'm into — ahh — into — meaningful relationships!

CYNTHIA. Friendship! Right. Sex isn't enough by itself. (*Quickly.*) At least I can't imagine that it would be.

MATT. A momentary flash of ecstasy. And then what?

CYNTHIA. The void. The slump. The letdown. (*Fast.*) At least, that's what I hear.

MATT. One minute you're in the sack, and the next you're . . .

CYNTHIA. In the pits — the dumps — the depths — the funkies. (*She smiles at him.*)

MATT. (*Smiling back at her.*) Postcoital depression. (*They smile blissfully at each other.*)

CYNTHIA. I do admire your vocabulary. That's precisely it. (*Slowly, savoring it.*) Postcoital depression. (*They gaze dreamily into each other's eyes.*)

MATT. (*Husky-voiced; mesmerized.*) You have beautiful eyes. And a beautiful voice. Say it again.

CYNTHIA. (*Slowly, sounding breathily sexy.*) Post . . . coital . . . depression . . .

MATT. (*Overcome with emotion.*) Wow . . . (*He gets up, aching from the physical ecstacy he feels; moves away from* CYNTHIA, *hardly able to walk.*)

CYNTHIA. (*Still breathy; gazing at him; full of emotion.*) Unless there's—something else . . .

MATT. (*Back turned, bending over slightly, to subdue his physical passion.*) Something—else?

CYNTHIA. Something special—that enhances it—both before *and* after.

MATT. (*Turning to her; sounding throaty.*) Oh . . . Yes . . . Friendship. Mutual interests. Like—overpopulation. And—sexual—repression.

CYNTHIA. (*Still looking at him, in awe.*) You have such wide-ranging ideas. (*Sultry-voiced.*) Such impressive—statistics. Such broad—shoulders.

MATT. Well, I told you, I'm a heavy reader.

CYNTHIA. (*Continuing to gaze at him with admiration.*) It shows. (*Worried,* MATT *looks down.*) You are so—different.

MATT. You think so? (*He quickly sits down in the nearest chair, crosses his legs.*)

CYNTHIA. I know so. Other men would have been plunging into it by now. (*Hastily.*) I mean, other men with other women! But we're both . . . Um . . . What's the word?

MATT. Abstemious. (*He sighs.*)

CYNTHIA. (*Disappointed.*) Oh? I was thinking more along the lines of—a happy medium.

MATT. Moderation—is that it?

CYNTHIA. (*Delighted.*) That's it, exactly. "*Le secret de la vie*," as Montaigne put it.

MATT. The secret of life—moderation. His best essay, don't you think?

CYNTHIA. Yes! You know, you really are an expert conversationalist.

MATT. I'm a conservationist, too.

CYNTHIA. You *are*? That's sensational! So am I.

MATT. Protecting dolphins is my specialty. (*He carefully picks up the dolphin figurine.*)

CYNTHIA. I can't believe it—that's my specialty, too! (*She picks up the toy stuffed whale, waves it, enthusiastic.*) Along with saving whales! And whooping cranes! And sequoias, and everything—including string! And preserving wetlands, and preventing forest fires . . . I don't even smoke, do you?

MATT. Well, I'm afraid I do—now and then. But I've been trying to . . .

CYNTHIA. (*Cutting in.*) Oh! That is, now and then!

MATT. I've been trying to quit, but I . . .

CYNTHIA. (*Fast.*) Quit? Me, too! . . . And I don't drink. Do you?

MATT. Well, as a matter of fact—sometimes, on special occasions, at parties . . .

CYNTHIA. (*Quickly.*) Oh! Except on special occasions! Like now! What would you like?

MATT. Anything! I mean . . . Just a little something to sip. Let me get it.

CYNTHIA. Let me—you won't be able to find it. (*She starts for the kitchen door.*)

MATT. I know my way around a kitchen.

CYNTHIA. (*Pleased; stopping, to let him go.*) You're unbelievable! The glasses are right here.

MATT. (*Exiting to the kitchen.*) You get the glasses. I'll get the booze. What'll you have?

CYNTHIA. Uh . . . Surprise me! (*She goes to the cabinet to get two glasses, and cocktail napkins.*)

MATT. (*Still calling from offstage.*) One surprise coming up. Very well stacked, uh, stocked! And everything's sparkling! Spotless! Not a dirty dish in the sink.

CYNTHIA. (*To herself, a little prayer; polishing the glasses vigorously.*) Oh, please don't let him look in the oven. (*She calls to him.*) Would you mind turning off my yogurt maker while you're out there? It's on the cupboard, next to the alfalfa sprouter. (*She puts the glasses and napkins on the coffee table.*)

MATT. (*From offstage.*) Sure . . . How?

CYNTHIA. You flip the switch to "Off." (*A metallic-sounding crash from offstage.*)

MATT. Done! (MATT *re-enters, looking comic, wearing a flamboyant, colorful, highly decorated, tourist type of Mexican sombrero. He holds both hands behind his back.*) Surprise! *Ole!*

CYNTHIA. Oh! (*She laughs at him with delight.*)

MATT. And here's another surprise! (*He shows her a bottle of tequila.*) *Ole!* Tequila happens to be one of my favorites—especially with fresh limes. (*He reveals a bowl with five limes in it.*) Say when! (*He opens the bottle, poises it over a glass.*)

CYNTHIA. None for me, thanks.

MATT. You mind if I . . .

CYNTHIA. Please! Go ahead.

MATT. (*Pouring himself a glass of tequila.*) Why'd you buy it? If you don't drink it.

CYNTHIA. Because I was in Mexico. And that's what you buy when you're in Mexico. Because it's cheap in Mexico.

MATT. All the way to Mexico, to get cheap booze? (*He sips his drink.*)

CYNTHIA. Well—I might as well be honest with you. I may be a computer programmer to earn my living. (*Confidential; this revelation is very special to her.*) But my secret passion is—lepidoptera.

MATT. I never would have guessed!

CYNTHIA. Don't get me wrong! I don't collect them—I'd never put a pin through a single one. But I love to watch them on the wing, in the sun and the flowers. So—I joined the Insect Migration Association, and on my last vacation, I went to Mexico to be a butterfly spotter.

MATT. A butterfly what?

CYNTHIA. (*With pride.*) I helped observe the winter bedroom of our monarch butterflies.

MATT. Sounds like fun. (*He laughs, sips his drink.*)

CYNTHIA. (*Full of excitement.*) It was! It's in the mountains, north of Mexico City. There they were— millions of them, hanging from the pine branches, a big beautiful blaze of orange! Those tiny fragile things fly all that way, from the eastern part of the U.S.A.—three thousand miles! And always to the same place, the same time, every year!

MATT. (*Watching* CYNTHIA, *entranced.*) Like the swallows coming back to Capistrano.

CYNTHIA. Instinct. Isn't it amazing?

MATT. Sure is. I'm a bird watcher myself. Birds and butterflies are almost all instinct. (*Still gazing at her,* MATT *starts to pour himself another drink, misses the glass.*)

CYNTHIA. (*Pleasant, unconcerned; wiping up the spill with a napkin.*) But not people. We've learned to suppress it—haven't we?

MATT. (*Concentrating on pouring his drink.*) Not a hundred percent. (MATT *takes a gulp of tequila, begins to sound intoxicated.*) Sometimes it just won't be suppressed. And maybe that's just as well. (*He moves beside* CYNTHIA *on the sofa.*) Maybe sometimes we should be more like the birds, and the butterflies. (*He puts his arm on the back of the sofa, behind* CYNTHIA'S *shoulders, his voice getting husky.*) And follow where our instinct leads us. (*He shuts his eyes, turns to kiss* CYNTHIA.)

CYNTHIA. (*With a smile; slipping away from* MATT.) Maybe we should!

MATT. (*Kissing empty air, opening his eyes; trying to cover his embarrassment.*) Say, did you by any chance bring back some music from Mexico?

CYNTHIA. A couple of tapes, for the memory. I prefer Bach, though.

MATT. I dig Bach in the morning. But not for celebrating.

CYNTHIA. Celebrating?

MATT. Your rescue.

CYNTHIA. (*Smiling at him.*) Oh, yes! My hero! (*She crosses to the stereo.*)

MATT. Let's drink to it. (*He pours tequila into the second glass, and refills his own.*)

CYNTHIA. No, thanks. I don't like the taste. (*The music comes on, a lively popular Mexican tune, with guitars, castanets, maracas.*)

MATT. (*With a Mexican accent; still wearing the Mexican sombrero.*) Zat's because you haven't tried eet zee Mexican way. (*He drains his glass, then flourishes two limes, swaying to the beat of the music.*) Weeth zee lime and zee salt.

CYNTHIA. Zee lime and zee salt?

MATT. (*Flinging the Mexican serape over his shoulder; Mexican accent.*) *Si, Si, señorita!* Tequila lovers always drink eet zat way—zee native way! *Ole!* (*Happily tipsy, he trills loud and high, Mexican style, and stamps his feet, doing a hip-swiveling Mexican kind of dance.*) *Mira!* Eet's zee only way to drink zee tequila! You see, all zee time zee tequila ees quenching your thirst, zee lime and zee salt are making you thirsty again! So drinking tequila—zee Mexican way—ees a continuous, never-ending process of tan-ta-li-zing and sa-tis-fy-ing and tan-ta-li-zing and sa-tis-fy-ing and tan-ta-li-zing and . . .

CYNTHIA. (*Cutting in; smiling; watching him.*) It sounds lewd to me.

MATT. (*Still dancing merrily; continuing to use the Mexican accent.*) Eet sounds what?

CYNTHIA. It looks lewd, too! (*She giggles.*)

MATT. Lewd? Zees looks lewd? (*He gives a bump and grind.*)

CYNTHIA. Yes! It looks lewd! (*She laughs.*)

MATT. Eet's supposed to! Come on, try eet! *Arriba! Arriba!*

CYNTHIA. I can't. I'd feel silly.

MATT. (*Grabbing her, trying to dance with her, gyrating wildly.*) Come on, Cyn! Party! Party! Let eet all hang out! Let yourself go!

CYNTHIA. Pull yourself together! (*Annoyed, she breaks away, turns off the music.*)

MATT. Here ees what you need—tequila! (*He hands* CYNTHIA *the second glass of tequila.*)

CYNTHIA. But I don't like it.

MATT. *Por favor, señorita,* taste eet—for me.

CYNTHIA. Well . . . (*She takes a big gulp, coughs.*)

MATT. (*Sounding more and more drunk.*) *Caramba!* Eet's supposed to be sipped. Slowly. Sipping satisfies certain psycho-biological needs you have.

CYNTHIA. Of course. Everybody needs liquids. (*She coughs, and finishes off the glass.*)

MATT. (*Tilting the sombrero down over one eye, approaching her slowly, staggering a bit from the tequila; suggestive.*) Eet's your lips, too.

CYNTHIA. (*Warily backing away from him.*) What about my lips?

MATT. (*Low-voiced; sexy.*) Your lips—need—sips. And zat brings us to . . . (*He reaches for her.*)

CYNTHIA. Oh, no, you don't! (CYNTHIA *angrily pushes* MATT *away.*)

MATT. (*Surprised; losing his balance; no longer using the Mexican accent.*) Hey! I was reaching for the limes! (*He laughs.*)

CYNTHIA. The limes? Well, here you are! (*She throws a lime at him, then another.*)

MATT. Oh! So you want a friendly fight, do you? A small struggle? (*He grabs for her.*)

CYNTHIA. Don't touch me! (*She tries to avoid his grasp, circling the room.*)

MATT. A tiny tussle? A giggly little quarrel? (*Poking at her.*) With a poke—and a push—and a pinch . . . (*He pinches her, laughs drunkenly.*)

CYNTHIA. *Ouch!*

MATT. I liked that! (*He tries to hug her.*)

CYNTHIA. Leave me alone! (*She grabs the bottle, brandishes it.*)

MATT. Hey, wait a minute! Bottles? A pitched battle? This is a celebration, isn't it? Or have you decided to join the revolution? With the nine-year-old nymphets! (*He laughs.*)

CYNTHIA. (*Still brandishing the bottle.*) As far as I'm concerned, it's total war.

MATT. Want to call a truce? I'm game for that, too. Lay down those arms, and we'll kiss and—make out. (*A laugh.*) Come on, Cyn—all the way!

CYNTHIA. Don't you understand? I DON'T WANT TO!

MATT. So that's what you are—a teaser.

CYNTHIA. I'm not teasing. Conversation, remember?

Moderation!

MATT. A tease, a fluff, a bluff! In that case, I'll have to let you have it. (*He starts for her, unsteady on his feet.*)

CYNTHIA. Don't you take another step! (*She moves away, holding the bottle ready.*)

MATT. Just what a little teaser needs. Something to juice her up! So she won't be so flat! So bland! (*Laughing drunkenly, he stumbles past her, picks up two limes.*)

CYNTHIA. I am NOT FLAT! (*She slams the bottle down on the table and storms off, into the kitchen.*)

MATT. (*Tipsy, grinning, holding up a lime in each hand.*) Lime juice! To make her more zippy, more tangy, more TART! (*Laughing raucously, he falls onto the floor pillows.*)

CYNTHIA. (*From offstage; furious.*) TART! OH! (*A metallic-sounding crash from offstage, as before.*)

MATT. Hey, Cyn! It's just a little juicy humor on my part. Just a juicy little joke. Don't you get it? (*He laughs merrily, takes out a small pocketknife, cuts the tips from two limes.*)

CYNTHIA. (*Shouting angrily from offstage.*) Insulting a person is not a little joke!

MATT. (*Calling to her.*) Blame it on the tequila. (*He laughs.*)

CYNTHIA. (*Continuing to shout from offstage.*) Ignoring civilized behavior is not a little joke!

MATT. It was your tequila. (*He crawls over to the table, gets the tequila bottle.*)

CYNTHIA. Taking advantage of an intoxicated woman . . .

MATT. It really hit the spot, didn't it? (*He refills the two glasses.*)

CYNTHIA. (*Still from offstage; her voice sounding*

upset, tearful.) When her defenses are down . . .

MATT. How about another slug? (*He takes a gulp of his tequila.*)

CYNTHIA. (*Re-entering; near tears; carrying a bowl of crackers and a bowl of cheese dip.*) You can't just walk into someone's home, and—and *violate* her. (*She sniffles.*)

MATT. What? Hey . . .

CYNTHIA. Just like your friend Harold Buckmaster! And then call it a little joke. (*She chokes back tears.*)

MATT. I didn't do that.

CYNTHIA. And hurt her feelings. Just like your friend Harold Buckmaster. (*She begins to cry.*)

MATT. Aw, Cyn—don't. Come on, cheer up. (*He mimics a donkey, fingers up for ears.*) Eeee-aw! Eeee-aw!

CYNTHIA. And you! . . .

MATT. (*Imitating a gorilla, tongue over upper teeth, hunched, scratching his sides, stalking about.*) Unh! Unh! Unh! Unh! Unh! (*He continues the gorilla act.*)

CYNTHIA. (*Starting to laugh in spite of herself.*) You're bananas! (*She laughs harder, wiping her tears.*)

MATT. Good! Go ahead—laugh! Join the party! Have a drink! (*He hands her her glass of tequila, picks up his own.*)

CYNTHIA. (*Reluctantly taking the glass.*) I don't like this stuff.

MATT. That's the spirit! (*Again using the Mexican accent.*) You'll like eet when you savor eet—zee Mexican way. (MATT *toasts* CYNTHIA, *takes a sip of his tequila.* CYNTHIA *warily takes a sip, rolls it around her mouth, crosses to sit on the floor pillows. Enjoying it, she takes another sip, then another.* MATT *crosses to her, hiding the two cut limes behind his back; no longer using the*

Mexican accent.) You happen to be talking to a champion.

CYNTHIA. Champion what?

MATT. (*Displaying a lime in each hand.*) Lime sucker!

CYNTHIA. Oh! (*Giggling, tipsy, she drains her glass, and grabs the tequila bottle.*)

MATT. You see, sucking is like sipping. It also satisfies certain . . . (*Having trouble getting the word out.*) psychobiological needs I have.

CYNTHIA. I have them, too! (*She giggles, takes gulps from the tequila bottle.*)

MATT. We all have them! Remember your butterflies? You know what they do with nectar?

CYNTHIA. Suck it! (*She goes into a fit of giggles.*)

MATT. Well, Cyn, that takes care of the preliminaries. You sip the tequila, you suck the lime, and now it's time for the *climax!*

CYNTHIA. (*Stops laughing abruptly; quickly puts down the bottle.*) Now just a minute!

MATT. (*After a moment.*) The salt. (*He laughs.*)

CYNTHIA. Oh! The salt! The salt! (*A giggle.*) You mean—the salt! (*A tipsy laugh.*) All you have to do is tell me when you want it! The salt, I mean. (*Gales of drunken laughter.*)

MATT. I just want to be sure you've got it.

CYNTHIA. (*Excited.*) I've got it, I've got it! Lots! Oodles! All you can use! . . . But when you get it . . . That is, when I come up with it . . . What are you going to do with it?

MATT. Lick it.

CYNTHIA. (*Shrieking and laughing.*) Aaaaaeeeeeeeeeeee!

MATT. What's the matter? What else can you do, besides—lick it?

CYNTHIA. (*Screaming with laughter.*) Eeeeee!

MATT. It's instinct. Animal instinct. Didn't you ever see an animal licking . . .

CYNTHIA. (*Cutting in; shrieking.*) NO! (*She giggles into the toy stuffed whale.*)

MATT. . . . salt at a salt lick?

CYNTHIA. (*Finally letting go.*) Ohhh! I wish I could! (*She laughs, happily drunk, exuberant.*) Oooo! I'd love to see a stag—or a stallion—licking salt at a salt lick! Tall! Strong! Erect! (*She laughs with delight.*)

MATT. (*With drunken jubilation.*) Wild! Free! Uninhibited! Pure instinct! Nobody has to teach a buck what to do. He knows where to go, all right. And he goes! And he knows what to do when he gets there. And he does it!

CYNTHIA. And I'll bet he likes it. I had a kitten once—her name was Patsy. And she liked it a lot.

MATT. Tame or wild, we all like it! (*Howling like a wolf.*) Ah-ooo!

CYNTHIA. Me-oww! Maybe that's why . . . (*She smiles.*)

MATT. Why—what?

CYNTHIA. Why ice-cream cones are so popular! (*She laughs.*)

MATT. Yeah! With an ice-cream cone you can just go to it!

CYNTHIA. Right on the street! Night or day! Eyes open or closed!

MATT. You can really get away with it with cones! Or popsicles!

CYNTHIA. Or postage stamps! Or anything that's salty! Pretzels—or popcorn—or peanuts—or potato chips! Or pickles! (*A giggle.*) Lick, lick, lick, lick, lick! I'm thirsty! More tequila, please.

MATT. Not till we get the salt. Where's the salt?

CYNTHIA. Oh, yes! The salt! (*Raucous laugh.*) Oooo! What fun! What a party! (*Singing.*) "La cucaracha! La cucaracha! . . ." (*Still singing,* CYNTHIA *runs to turn on the stereo, then exits to the kitchen. Mexican music is heard, as before.* MATT *turns the lights low, arranges the tequila bottle, the glasses, and the cut limes at the floor pillow area, sits down there, and refills the two glasses with tequila.* CYNTHIA *re-enters; waving a large salt shaker; singing, loud, drunk, happy; dancing over to him, to the music.*) "South of the bor-der! Down May-hee-co way! . . ." Here's the salt!

MATT. And here's the limes!

CYNTHIA. And here's the tequila! (*She laughs, sits down on a pillow across from* MATT.)

MATT. Now you're going to find out how they all go together to make a total effect that is absolutely—fantastic! (*He shakes some salt onto the back of her hand.*) Or, as the saying goes where the lime tree grows—(*Rolling the "r".*) Forrrr-mee-dah-blay! (*He shakes salt onto the back of his own hand.*) How the first ingredient makes you thirst for it! (*He licks the salt from his hand.*)

CYNTHIA. Thirst! (*Watching him, she licks the salt from her hand.*)

MATT. How the next one rouses the appetite! (*He sucks his lime.*)

CYNTHIA. Rouses! Umm! (*She sucks her lime.*)

MATT. How the next one excites the senses! (*He tosses down his drink.*)

CYNTHIA. Excites! (CYNTHIA *tosses down her drink.* MATT *refills the two glasses, shakes more salt on their hands. The Mexican music continues to play. They speak faster and louder.*)

MATT. And stimulates! (*He licks the salt from his hand.*)

CYNTHIA. Stimulates! (*She licks the salt from her hand.*)

MATT. And tantalizes! (*He sucks his lime.*)

CYNTHIA. Tantalizes! (*She sucks her lime.*)

MATT. And titillates! (*He drinks.*)

CYNTHIA. Titillates! (*She drinks.*)

MATT. Making you want more! (*He licks more salt, refills the two glasses.*)

CYNTHIA. More! (*She licks more salt.*)

MATT. And more! (*He sucks his lime, downs the tequila.*)

CYNTHIA. And more! (*She sucks her lime, downs her tequila.*)

MATT. (*Getting up; starting to do his Mexican dance.*) So you go on and on!

CYNTHIA. (*Getting up; imitating* MATT'S *Mexican dance.*) And on and on! (MATT *grabs* CYNTHIA, *dances with her.*)

MATT. Sipping and sucking and licking!

CYNTHIA. And sipping and sucking and licking! (*They go on dancing together, more and more wildly.*)

MATT. Over and over!

CYNTHIA. And over and over!

MATT. *Arriba!*

CYNTHIA. *Arriba!*

MATT. Around!

CYNTHIA. And around!

MATT. Dipping and dipping! (*Still dancing,* MATT "*dips*" CYNTHIA.)

CYNTHIA. And dipping and dipping!

MATT. Up!

CYNTHIA. And up!

MATT. Down! (*He "dips" her again.*)

CYNTHIA. And down! Whee!

MATT. And down . . . (*Looking sick, groaning,* MATT *lets* CYNTHIA *drop gently to the floor at the end of the "dip."*) Ohh . . . All of a sudden—I feel sick. (*He reels around, holding his stomach.*)

CYNTHIA. (*Getting up off the floor; exuberant.*) Up, and up! (*She grabs the serape, whirls it around.*) Whee!

MATT. (*Moaning; groping his way to the sofa.*) Ohh . . .

CYNTHIA. Come on! Join in! Let yourself go!

MATT. No . . . (*He falls onto the sofa; the sombrero falls off.*)

CYNTHIA. (*Dancing alone, faster, waving the serape.*) Round and round! In and out! Come on! In and out! And up and down! And in and out!

MATT. Don't say that. Please. (*Groaning; nauseous.*) Ohh . . .

CYNTHIA. *Arriba, arriba!* (*She puts on the sombrero, trills on a high note, Mexican style, dances wildly.*) Forrrr-mee-dah-blay! Hey, party-pooper! Join in! Forrrr-mee-dah-blay!

MATT. For-mee-dah . . . (*Trying not to retch.*) . . . blaaggh . . . I'm dizzy . . .

CYNTHIA. (*Stamping, dancing with joyful abandon.*) All the way! (*The Mexican music plays on, but softer.*)

MATT. (*Flat on his back on the sofa, holding his head.*) All the way . . . Very dizzy . . .

CYNTHIA. (*Using the serape, going at* MATT *like a bull-fighter.*) Hey! Toro! *Ole! Ole!*

MATT. Oh, hell . . .

CYNTHIA. O-*lay!* (*She falls on top of him on the sofa, laughing.*)

MATT. (*Gasping.*) Ufff! No . . . Keep your o-lays to yourself.

CYNTHIA. Aw, Chico, o-*lays* are meant for two. (*She

kisses him.)

MATT. (*Sounding sick.*) Not now. I had too much tequila. And so did you.

CYNTHIA. Sure, we're celebrating, aren't we?

MATT. Not any more. (*He feebly tries to push her away.*)

CYNTHIA. (*Pinning his arms back, sounding very drunk.*) Lay down those arms, and we'll kiss, and—make out.

MATT. (*Moaning.*) Ohh . . . I don't feel—up to it.

CYNTHIA. Come on, Matt Matthews! All the way!

MATT. Forget it. Ohhh . . .

CYNTHIA. So that's what you are—a teaser!

MATT. I'm not teasing. I'm sick. Ohhh . . . (*He tries to sit up.*)

CYNTHIA. A tease, a fluff, a bluff! In that case . . . (*Pushing him back down.*) I'll have to let you have it.

MATT. (*Unable to resist; weakly.*) No! . . . Help . . .

CYNTHIA. (*Laughing tipsily, loosening his tie, opening the top of his shirt.*) Just what a big tease deserves.

MATT. Stop . . . I can't . . .

CYNTHIA. Just a pinch . . . (*She tweaks his nose.*)

MATT. Ouch!

CYNTHIA. To spice him up. All you can do is submit to your fate. (*Deep, gruff voice.*) Like a man.

MATT. This is rape!

CYNTHIA. (*Straddling him.*) No, this isn't rape. But go ahead—scream rape, if it turns you on.

MATT. Rape, rape! (*He covers his face with his arms.*)

CYNTHIA. You'd sound kind of silly screaming, "Mutual consent!" (*She laughs happily, begins to shake salt onto his neck.*)

MATT. Don't . . . (*A giggle.*) That tickles. (*He laughs.*)

CYNTHIA. Of course. I'm salting you. (*She goes on shaking salt over his body, from neck to foot.*)

MATT. You're what? (*He peeks through his arms.*)

CYNTHIA. Salting you. Disappointed?

MATT. (*Giggling, weakly trying to ward her off.*) Stop it.

CYNTHIA. It's just what a hung-over drunk needs—some salt. A little rub in the wound. (*Laughing, she rubs some salt into his ankle.*)

MATT. (*Struggling feebly.*) Cut it out . . . That's enough.

CYNTHIA. (*Shaking more salt on him.*) Not yet, Matthews. You're still too tasteless. Too limp. Too bland.

MATT. I am not limp!

CYNTHIA. (*Giving a tipsy laugh, still shaking salt over him.*) That's why you need more salt. To give you more flavor, more body! (*Sitting on top of the back of the sofa, she takes off her shoes.*)

MATT. (*Still lying exhausted, supine, on the sofa.*) You can't just jump right on top of a person, and practically . . . (*Shocked.*) Why are you taking your shoes off?

CYNTHIA. (*Standing up on the arm of the sofa, towering over* MATT.) Maybe you don't know what you want. (*She gleefully unbuttons her blouse.*) But I know what I want! (*She takes her blouse off; under it she wears a lacy slip.*)

MATT. I'm surprised at you! You think I'm a sex object? A plaything?

CYNTHIA. (*Swinging her blouse around.*) Afraid you won't be able to—swing it? (*She throws her blouse at him.*)

MATT. Cynthia! You can't do this!

CYNTHIA. I can, if you can! . . . Ready? (*She turns out the light. Blackout, or very dim light. Brief pause, as* CYNTHIA *gropes around the sofa.*) Hey! Where are you?

MATT. (*Crawling on his hands and knees toward the front door.*) Looking for the door. (*A loud crash as* MATT *knocks over a chair.*) *Ow!*

CYNTHIA. You can't leave me like this! (*She falls on top of* MATT *on the floor.*) Gotcha!

MATT. Let me go! (*They roll around the floor in the darkness. The music comes to a stop.*)

CYNTHIA. (*Hanging on to* MATT, *pleading passionately.*) Give me a chance, Matt, Please! (*She gives him a long, audible kiss, then sighs.*) Ohhh . . .

MATT. (*Giving a sigh.*) Ohhh . . . (*A pleased chuckle.*) Oh! (*A long sigh, succumbing.*) Ohhhh . . .Cyn . . . Ummm . . . (*Brief pause, as* CYNTHIA *quietly moves away.*) Cyn? Where'd you go? . . . Hey, it's all right . . . Cynthia! . . . I've changed my mind.

CYNTHIA. (*In the darkness, from across the room.*) So have I.

MATT. (*Disappointed.*) You have? (*Lights up, as* CYNTHIA *turns on a lamp; she is on the other side of the room from* MATT.)

CYNTHIA. (*Hastily putting her blouse back on.*) The tequila's wearing off, and I'm . . . Well—I'm scared.

MATT. (*Sprawled out on the floor, flat on his back, feeling the after-effects of the tequila.*) Of me? (*He tries to raise his head, lets it fall back on the floor.*)

CYNTHIA. (*Sounding somewhat resentful; smoothing her clothes and hair.*) I guess I can thank my mother for it. And my father. She always told me to save my . . . Well . . . And he told me to . . . To keep my legs crossed. And I did. Most of the time. I mean I didn't. Most of the time. Understand?

MATT. (*Still on his back, on the floor.*) Not exactly.

CYNTHIA. (*Brusquely straightening up the room as she talks.*) Let me put it this way . . . When I was a kid, I always looked old for my age. At ten, I looked twelve. At thirteen, I looked sixteen. So they were always after me — like at the party tonight. And I got . . . Well . . . It made me mad. They were all after the same thing — over and over. And who needs men, anyhow — right? (*With a quick look at* MATT.) Well, I mean . . . I do like guys, but . . .

MATT. Joe asked you out, and you told him to go fly a kite.

CYNTHIA. With his kids. Joe's married.

MATT. Oh. Well, Dennis asked you, and you told him to drop dead.

CYNTHIA. Dennis belongs to the Rifle Association. He shoots innocent ducks and bunny rabbits . . . You see, for some time now . . . Well, basically, I guess I've been saying "no" a lot. I tell myself it's — thoughtful and mature.

MATT. (*Still on the floor; sitting up slowly.*) Sounds familiar. I was seventeen before I got up enough nerve to . . . And then I bungled it. And I bungled it the next time, too. And then I . . . I tried to convince myself — well — that there was nothing wrong with being a lonely wolf. Anyway, I turned more and more to — books. Until . . .

CYNTHIA. Until?

MATT. (*Getting up on his feet with some difficulty.*) Cynthia, I have a confession to make. This didn't just happen.

CYNTHIA. I know it didn't.

MATT. (*Earnest.*) I mean . . . I saw you the first day you walked through the portals of Frick and Frick. And for weeks, I've been observing you from a distance—behind the filing cabinets, over the water fountain . . . I even followed you home once.

CYNTHIA. Once?

MATT. Fourteen times.

CYNTHIA. I noticed.

MATT. Oh.

CYNTHIA. It was somewhere between the fifth and the tenth time that I read your—file. (*She looks guilty.*)

MATT. What file?

CYNTHIA. Your—personnel file.

MATT. My personnel file? That's personal! I haven't even seen it myself.

CYNTHIA. What do you want to know?

MATT. How'd I do on the polygraph test?

CYNTHIA. Why ask? You're a hundred percent honest. That's one reason I wanted to meet you—and your mother. (*Trying to hide her regret.*) I think it's so sweet that your mother lives with you.

MATT. She lives with my father. In North Dakota.

CYNTHIA. But in your lie-detector test, you said . . .

MATT. I lied! . . . I had to—so I could qualify for a two-bedroom apartment. I have three thousand, six hundred, seventy-nine books. And fifty-four plants. And—a poodle.

CYNTHIA. A poodle! A poodle?

MATT. Don't you like dogs?

CYNTHIA. Your mother's a poodle? I mean—the poodle's your mother? Terrific! That is . . . It was wrong of me, I admit. But there I was, day after day, alone with Martha—Martha's my computer. And she was bursting with information about you. I just couldn't stop myself—or Martha—once she got started. She told me everything. And everything was so spectacular! You're so typical! I mean, you're so special! You're average! You're unique! (*Catching herself, embarrassed.*) I guess I should apologize for invading your privacy like that.

MATT. (*Gathering up his courage, facing her across the room.*) Cynthia, Martha didn't tell you everything. (*Watching her closely; apprehensive.*) Last Thursday I worked out a little deal with Harold. Harold—Buckmaster.

CYNTHIA. No!

MATT. (*Sheepish.*) That's why he did—what he did—at the party tonight. (*Worried.*) What *did* he do, anyhow?

CYNTHIA. You put Harold up to it? (*Surprise turns to anger.*) Why, that rotten, underhanded . . .

MATT. I told him to take it easy!

CYNTHIA. And you! . . . (*She abruptly bursts into laughter.*) Oh, it's just too much!

MATT. Gosh, I'm glad you can laugh about it now. I hope he didn't go too far. (*Anxious.*) Did he?

CYNTHIA. In a way. Yesterday Mr. Harold Buckmaster came to me with what sounded like an ingenious plan . . . And I agreed to it.

MATT. (*Astounded.*) You? And Harold? You two planned—the same thing? . . . (MATT *stands stunned, speechless for a moment, then begins to laugh.* CYNTHIA *laughs with him.*) Well, it seems we do have a lot in common. You're a sneak and a liar, just like me.

CYNTHIA. And abstemious, just like you.

MATT. And ready for a change, just like me.

CYNTHIA. A change?

MATT. Well, we got started, didn't we? Here I am. (*They stand, looking across the room at each other.*)

CYNTHIA. Yes. Here you are, aren't you? Right here.

MATT. And you, too. Here we are.

CYNTHIA. Both of us. Just — communicating away — aren't we?

MATT. (*Moving a few steps closer to her.*) In spite of everything. Word after word, idea after idea.

CYNTHIA. (*Moving a step or two closer to him.*) And listening, too! Listening is half of a conversation, isn't it? Maybe more than half. (*Smiling shyly at him.*) By the way, you're a wonderful listener, Matt.

MATT. (*Smiling nervously at her.*) Thank you. So are you. And a wonderful talker, as well.

CYNTHIA. Am I? Really? Why, thank you! You are, too.

MATT. (*Moving another step closer to her.*) And putting them together — talking and listening, listening and talking — sometimes leads two people to find . . .

CYNTHIA. Friendship. (*She moves another step closer to him.*)

MATT. A meaningful relationship.

CYNTHIA. One mutual interest after another. They love to talk.

MATT. (*Moving a step closer to her.*) And they love to read.

CYNTHIA. (*Moving a step closer to him.*) And they love to watch birds, and save dolphins.

MATT. And they love to dance.

CYNTHIA. And they love to . . . They love . . . Oh . . .

MATT and CYNTHIA. (*Almost simultaneous; ecstatic.*) I love you, Cynthia!

I love you, Matt!

(*They rush together, fall into each other's arms, and kiss, whirling, tumbling over the back of the sofa, down onto it, arms and legs every which way.*)

CYNTHIA. Oh! Oh! Oh! Oh! . . . We said it! (*Astonished, overjoyed, tangled together on the sofa, hugging tightly, they look into each other's eyes.*) We said it . . .

MATT. I want to say it again.

CYNTHIA. Oh, I could listen forever . . . I want to say it again, too.

MATT. I think we're onto something — precoital elation. (*Howling like a wolf.*) Ah-ooo! Beauty and the beast. (*Still awkwardly entwined with* CYNTHIA *on the sofa,* MATT *kisses her, a long tender kiss.*)

CYNTHIA. (*Singing; smiling.*) "You found a girl . . ." (MATT *joins in the song.*)

MATT and CYNTHIA. (*Singing together; smiling; looking into each other's eyes.*) ". . . just like the girl that married dear old dad . . ." (*As they sing, the lights dim to blackout.*)

END OF PLAY

SEDUCTION DUET

PROPERTY AND COSTUME PLOT

CYNTHIA

Dressy blouse, buttoned at the front
Full skirt
Lacy slip
Stylish shoes

MATT

Subdued suit
Dress shirt
Conservative tie
Small pocketknife in pants pocket

SET, ONSTAGE

Full-size sofa, with arms, center stage
   On the sofa:
   A Mexican serape, as a throw, over the back of it
   Several small sofa pillows
   A toy stuffed whale, two feet long
Two easy chairs, to each side of sofa
Coffee table, in front of sofa
   On the coffee table:
   A few books and magazines, including one on conserva-
     tion and one on butterflies
   A figurine of a dolphin
Two lamps, near the sofa and chairs
Stereo set, upstage right
Cabinet, upstage left, containing drinking glasses and
   cocktail napkins

Bookcases filled with books, at the sides of the set
Large framed print or photograph of a monarch butterfly, hanging on the back wall
A wall mirror, hanging near the front door, stage right
Several large floor pillows, as a seating area, down center left

PROPERTIES, OFFSTAGE

MATT
Mexican sombrero, flamboyant, colorful, highly decorated, tourist type
A full bottle of tequila
A bowl with five limes in it

CYNTHIA
A bowl of crackers
A bowl of cheese dip
A large salt shaker

SOUND

Tape of lively popular Mexican music, with guitars, castanets, maracas
Offstage metallic-sounding crash

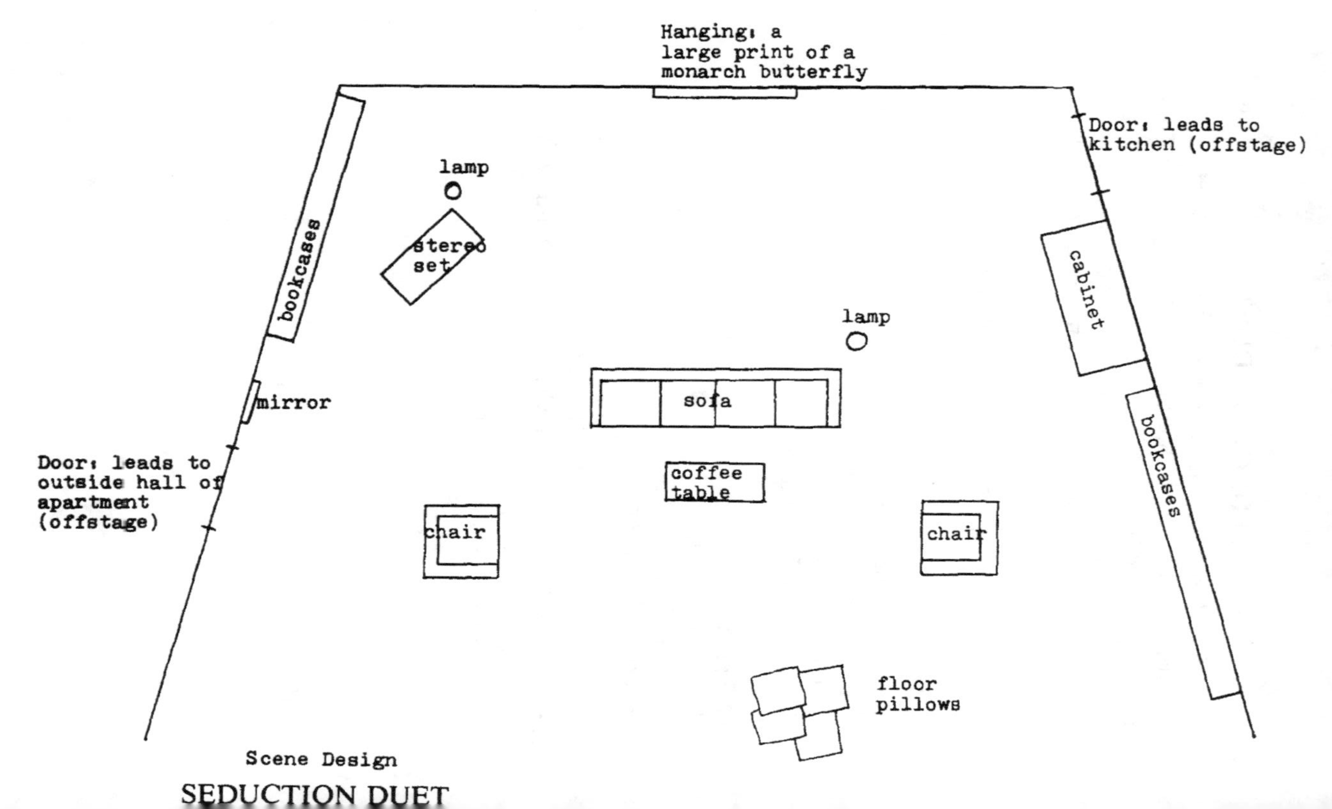

SEDUCTION DUET

A Bench at the Edge

A BENCH AT THE EDGE was presented by the Double Image Theatre at the Sixth Annual Off-Off Broadway Original Short Play Festival, St. Clement's Theatre, on May 27th, 1981, with the following cast:

(In order of appearance)

MAN ONE ....*Luigi Jannuzzi*
MAN TWO........................*Charles Downing*
BULLETS ....*Bill Wall*

Directed by Luigi Jannuzzi

Technical Coordinator, Gordon A. Juel

TIME: *The Present*

PLACE: *A bench at the edge of an abyss*

THE EDGE

"It doesn't have to be what it is when you first go there, though it is what it is when you're forced there, it is however, the children's knowledge of the place that forms the tears."

L.J.

In memory of my grandmother:
Mrs. Josephine Curcio

A Bench at the Edge

SET: *A bench at the edge of an abyss. The edge of the abyss is represented by the front edge of the stage and offstage right. All characters enter from offstage left.*

Lights rise on a bare stage with black background. We see MAN ONE *sitting on bench downstage right holding head in hands.* MAN ONE *has a long extension cord attached to him running from offstage left.*

MAN ONE *sits up hearing something, looks towards upstage left, stands, walks to center stage and peers into offstage wings. Surprised,* MAN ONE *then goes back to bench, and sits down slouching so as not to be seen by who is coming.*

MAN TWO *enters from stage left, talking to himself.*

MAN TWO. And I knew it. I knew it. I knew he was up there too. Why did I go up there? I knew he was going to be there with her. Ah. Who cares. (*On edge, talking to abyss.*) I should. I should, that would show them. (*Laughs.*) That would show them.

MAN ONE. Hey fella?

MAN TWO. (Two looks over.)

MAN ONE. Hi. (*Waving.*) Hello? (*Pause.*) Well, you could at least say hello, wave back or something. Come on, say hello. (*Waves again.*) Hello? Hi?

MAN TWO. (*Waves.*) Hello.

MAN ONE. Hey what's the matter with you? You're not surprised to see me or what? Huh?

MAN TWO. Surprised to see you?

MAN ONE. Yea, aren't you surprised to see me? No?

MAN TWO. (*Takes out, puts on glasses.*) Do . . . do I know you?

MAN ONE. Come here. Geez, . . . the least you can do is come over here for a minute and say hello. Come here, you can't even see me from there. Come over here.

MAN TWO. Where do I know you from?

MAN ONE. Geez, you'd think I had a gun or something. Come over here, come closer, come on get the full surprise.

MAN TWO. (*Walks over.*) I'm sorry but . . . you don't look familiar. Where do I know you from?

MAN ONE. Surprised huh? You're surprised aren't you? Huh? Life is full of surprises you know.

MAN TWO. But where have we met? I don't remember ever meeting you?

MAN ONE. Nowhere. You don't know me. You never met me.

MAN TWO. Then where do you know me from? How . . . how do you know me?

MAN ONE. I don't know you. What makes you think I know you?

MAN TWO. But you said I'd be surprised to see you here. I thought you said you knew me.

MAN ONE. I never said that. No, I never met you before in my life.

MAN TWO. Oh I thought you recognized me. You said I should be surprised to see you.

MAN ONE. Yea, I thought you'd be surprised to see anybody here. I mean, no one ever thinks he'll ever meet anybody here when they come here. I mean, did you?

MAN TWO. No. I never even thought about that.

MAN ONE. And who does? And the people here are so ashamed to be here, nobody even talks to anybody. But don't worry about it. I'll never tell anybody you were here, even if I do find out who you are. I never saw you here. I just wanted to talk to somebody and there you were.

MAN TWO. Well, that's friendly.

MAN ONE. I think so.

MAN TWO. Hello then.

MAN ONE. Hi.

MAN TWO. Well, it seems you've picked the right person. I'll talk to anybody. I mean, that doesn't bother me. I don't care who finds out I was here.

MAN ONE. Yea, sure. Who are you kidding? You don't care who finds out you were here.

MAN TWO. I don't. I don't care.

MAN ONE. Yea right. Come on, I saw what you're doing. I know what you're up to. You're looking at the abyss.

MAN TWO. Yes, yes I was. So what, I was looking at the abyss?

MAN ONE. (*To abyss.*) Giant, isn't it?

MAN TWO. Yes, it is. What do you mean you know what I'm up to?

MAN ONE. Frightening, isn't it?

MAN TWO. A bit. Huh? You don't know anything about me.

MAN ONE. Such a big nothing. Huge, so endless, just there, right there. It's something.

MAN TWO. Yes it is something. Are you going to answer my question or not?

MAN ONE. (*To* MAN TWO.) All right, I'll answer your question. Look, I know what you're here for, and I know what you're doing.

MAN TWO. Oh yea . . . what am I doing?

MAN ONE. I know.

MAN TWO. I'm just looking . . . walking. Just looking and walking.

MAN ONE. Yea. Sure, right. Listen buddy, you can't fool me. You might be able to fool other people, but not me. I know. I know why you're here, and what you're doing. (*Smiles.*) Suppose your neighbors found out about this, or your boss, or your insurance company? Huh? What do you think they'd do?

MAN TWO. I'm just looking.

MAN ONE. What do you take me for, a fool? I've been around here a long time.

MAN TWO. Then what am I doing? Why don't *you* tell me?

MAN ONE. You're thinking. Thinking. That's what you're doing.

MAN TWO. All right, I might be thinking, but I'm walking and looking. That's why I'm here.

MAN ONE. Wrong. You're thinking. That's the important thing here. That's what brings people here.

MAN TWO. All right, so maybe it does.

MAN ONE. You're contemplating. That's what you're doing.

MAN TWO. All right, so maybe I am. So what?

MAN ONE. Admit it. At least admit you're contemplating.

MAN TWO. All right, so I'm contemplating. So what?

MAN ONE. I know. You can't fool me, I know. You walk here often?

MAN TWO. No. No, this is my first time here.

MAN ONE. You sure of that?

MAN TWO. I should know shouldn't I, if it's my first time, if I ever walked here before? Why do you care *anyway?*

MAN ONE. (*Laughs.*)

MAN Two. What are you laughing about?

MAN ONE. That's funny.

MAN Two. What's funny?

MAN ONE. You. (*Laughs.*) You're trying so hard to prove you're not ashamed of being here. And I know you are.

MAN Two. I'm not.

MAN ONE. (*Laughs.*) Yea.

MAN Two. And what if I am? What business is it of yours even if I was?

MAN ONE. It's none of my business. But you're ashamed. I can see it. It's written all over your clenched teeth.

MAN Two. I'm not ashamed of being here, of looking, watching, thinking, of anything.

MAN ONE. What a liar.

MAN Two. Why should I be? I wanted to come here and I'm here.

MAN ONE. Liar.

MAN Two. Look, I don't know who you are, or what you're doing here, but to set this straight I came here, I wanted to come here—and you can tell anybody you please where I am, or what I'm going to do.

MAN ONE. You planned this out to be here?

MAN Two. Yea, well, kind of.

MAN ONE. Liar.

MAN Two. Well, no, I didn't plan this out. It . . . it just happened; circumstances brought me here, and I'm here.

MAN ONE. Suppose I told you a year ago you were going to be here? What would you have said? If I said you were going to be here next year? Huh?

MAN Two. Oh . . . (*Snicker.*) well . . . no, I . . . I wouldn't have believed you.

MAN ONE. Why not?

Man Two. Because . . . well.

Man One. Why not?

Man Two. Well, I just . . . I just never thought I'd ever do something like this, I'd ever think about doing something like this; I'd ever . . . be here.

Man One. That's why I thought you'd be ashamed.

Man Two. (*Pause.*) Okay. So maybe this isn't the most heroic thing to do. But it's my decision.

Man One. I didn't say it wasn't. But you must be surprised to be here.

Man Two. (*Snicker.*) Oh you bet I'm surprised I'm here.

Man One. Disappointed? Go on, be honest. I don't know you, you don't know me.

Man Two. (*Nods yes.*) Sure. Yea, I'm disappointed I'm here. Aren't you disappointed you're here?

Man One. Thought you were more of a man? Huh?

Man Two. No, maybe not more of a man.

Man One. More confident?

Man Two. (*Nods yes.*) Yea, maybe.

Man One. Stronger?

Man Two. Maybe that too. What about you?

Man One. More intelligent?

Man Two. I guess. (*Pause.*) Who are you anyway? What do you care?

Man One. I don't. I don't care. I just wondered.

Man Two. But who are you?

Man One. Nobody. I'm not telling you my name; I'm not asking yours. I just wanted to talk to somebody, and you walked by. You said you weren't ashamed to be here, and I figure if we're going to talk, we should at least be honest.

Man Two. That's true.

Man One. Honesty's a good policy.

MAN TWO. That's right. How about you? Are you ashamed of being here?

MAN ONE. Oh now, wait a second. I don't have to answer that.

MAN TWO. Why not? I answered yours.

MAN ONE. Ut uh.

MAN TWO. Why not, Why don't you have to answer that?

MAN ONE. I just don't.

MAN TWO. You ask me personal questions: Why I'm here, What I'm going to do, Am I ashamed to be here. I answered you. Now I ask you one question and you don't have to answer it?

MAN ONE. That's right.

MAN TWO. Well I know. I know just like you do *now*. You're ashamed of being here too. I mean, that's common sense, anybody who comes here has to be ashamed. Who was I fooling saying I wasn't. This is it, you know, this is it. This is the edge.

MAN ONE. You're wrong. I'm not ashamed to be here.

MAN TWO. Oh, come on.

MAN ONE. Nope. I'm not ashamed to be here.

MAN TWO. Don't play games with me. Everybody's ashamed that comes here and you know it. I mean . . . that's normal isn't it?

MAN ONE. There's exceptions. There are.

MAN TWO. Who in their right mind could ever picture themselves here?

MAN ONE. I'm not ashamed and I live here.

MAN TWO. You live here?

MAN ONE. Yup.

MAN TWO. How can you live here? That's impossible, there's no place to live.

MAN ONE. (*Smiles and stands.*) I do. This is my

bench, my personal bench. I paint it once a year, with my paint. And that's my favorite view of the whole abyss. And I've been all around the abyss. And it's big you know, about as big as the earth is round. And I've seen it all. Well, not all, not the abyss, just the edge. I know where the edge is. I've seen it in all conditions, different changes, conflicts, and it is my opinion—a personal opinion—but I believe this is the best view of the edge of the abyss. And that's why I live here. (*Sits.*)

MAN TWO. And you live here?

MAN ONE. Uh huh.

MAN TWO. On this bench?

MAN ONE. My bench.

MAN TWO. Your bench.

MAN ONE. Right.

MAN TWO. Watching the abyss.

MAN ONE. And the edge. Usually I just try to stare down into it, to get a sense of it, of blankness. It makes time nothing, just like it itself. It stops time, time doesn't exist down there.

MAN TWO. (*Pointing upstage left.*) How about going back there? Ever go back there?

MAN ONE. No, No, I don't even face that way.

MAN TWO. Never?

MAN ONE. Nope.

MAN TWO. When was the last time you tried it?

MAN ONE. I've tried it, believe me. That's why I face this way. No, I've got nothing over there. I used to, I used to turn the bench around. One month this way, one month that way, then two months this way, one month that, then three this, one that. Then I tried at least one month a year to face that way. None of them worked. I hate it over there. I don't belong over there. I even tried to turn around occasionally, but . . . no. (*Looks *around to upstage left.*) I can't look that way. It's too depressing. I don't fit in. There's nothing over there.

MAN TWO. (*To abyss.*) What's over there?

MAN ONE. (*Proudly.*) Nothing.

MAN TWO. (*Pointing upstage left.*) Then, well, at least there's something that way. There's something back there.

MAN ONE. No, but there isn't. That's not real. That's worst than nothing. There's something there that I can only pretend to be a part of. (*To abyss.*) This is honest, real. I can be like that someday, the way it is. Sometimes I sit, clear my mind, and I can feel the welcome, the warmth of it.

MAN TWO. You have nothing back there?

MAN ONE. No.

MAN TWO. Nothing?

MAN ONE. Nope.

MAN TWO. That's hard to believe. Everyone has something: a home, a car.

MAN ONE. I don't.

MAN TWO. Relatives?

MAN ONE. Nope. A hospital bed, a personal nurse, a few machines, some electrical wires, that's about it.

MAN TWO. You're in a hospital?

MAN ONE. Yea.

MAN TWO. Oh. I'm sorry.

MAN ONE. Where are you?

MAN TWO. I'm in my car, in the garage. The door's closed. I don't know whether to start my car.

MAN ONE. You're questioning. That's why you're here. I've seen enough people like you come here.

MAN TWO. Yea, well I am.

MAN ONE. You're wondering, right?

MAN TWO. Yea . . . That's what I'm doing.

MAN ONE. That's healthy. It is.

MAN TWO. I guess.

MAN ONE. It is, it's very healthy.

MAN TWO. Maybe it is, but . . . I . . . I feel guilty about it, about being here.

MAN ONE. Oh, the hell with that guilt stuff. Life is a short walk. (*Snicker.*) I don't mean that as a pun, but, it is. It's a short walk. Seventy years or so as an average and that's it. Boom, the final gun, it's over. And some people stop once in a while and try to figure out if it's worth it. It's good to think the way you're thinking.

MAN TWO. I guess.

MAN ONE. It is.

MAN TWO. And this is worth it to you? To be here, to sit here like this?

MAN ONE. To be honest, I have no choice. Does that answer your question?

MAN TWO. Oh. I'm sorry.

MAN ONE. But the edge is honest. It's easy. It makes it very easy.

MAN TWO. Oh, that's why you don't feel guilty.

MAN ONE. Of course. I have no guilt at all. There's no reason I should feel guilty being here. I live here. I'm here constantly.

MAN TWO. I see.

MAN ONE. And that's why I'm not ashamed.

MAN TWO. That's right. There would be no reason to be.

MAN ONE. None.

MAN TWO. I see.

MAN ONE. It's simple. Isn't it.

MAN TWO. (*Nods yes.*) But not for me it's not. If somebody were to find out I was here—I don't know. That's why I was . . . I was so surprised when you said hello. I thought you recognized me, you knew me. I would never . . . I couldn't ever tell anyone, not even my wife. (*Laughs.*) She'd probably just use it in court against me.

MAN ONE. I've been here twenty-five years.

MAN TWO. Twenty-five years?

MAN ONE. Yup.

MAN TWO. No—how long have you been here?

MAN ONE. Twenty-five years. Why would I lie? I have no reason to lie. I have no reason to do anything.

MAN TWO. And you just sit here?

MAN ONE. Twenty-five years.

MAN TWO. And look, and stare?

MAN ONE. Yea. I look. Like I explained to you. I look into the abyss.

MAN TWO. For twenty-five years?

MAN ONE. I used to think. Thank God that's over. Whoops. (*Smiles.*) Sorry. I try not to say that. Reminds me of back there too much. (*Suddenly stands and wide eyed, eyes darting toward upstage left, listening.*)

MAN TWO. What's the matter?

MAN ONE. Shh. . . .

MAN TWO. By the way, what's the cord for?

MAN ONE. Shh. Listen.

MAN TWO. What's that cord attached to you for?

MAN ONE. Shh . . . Get behind me.

MAN TWO. What?

MAN ONE. Just get behind me. I'll explain it later.

MAN TWO. What's going on?

MAN ONE. Someone's coming.

MAN TWO. Who's coming? And what's the cord for?

MAN ONE. Sometimes they don't know what they're doing. Get behind me. (MAN TWO *gets behind* MAN ONE.) Now if you listen to me you won't get hurt.

Man Two. Who doesn,t know what they're doing?

Man One. You'll see. Shh . . .

Man Two. What's going on? What're you listening for?

Man One. Listen. (*They listen.*) You hear that?

Man Two. What?

Man One. Listen. (*They listen.*) Over there.

Man Two. I don't hear anything.

Man One. You don't hear that?

Man Two. What? What am I listening for?

Man One. Footsteps.

Man Two. And you hear them?

Man One. Running. Listen. (*They listen.*) Hear them?

Man Two. No.

Man One. Running this way. At us. Well not "at us."

Man Two. I don't . . . (*Eyes widen, he hears it.*) Oh yea. I hear it. (*Audience hears it too, a scream of anger.*)

Man One. It's one of them.

Man Two. Who?

Man One. We have to be ready for this. Get ready for this. Get behind me.

Man Two. Is this guy after you?

Man One. No.

Man Two. But you know who it is?

Man One. How am I suppose to know who it is? Now listen to me: They don't know what they're doing, you understand?

Man Two. Uh huh. Who's they?

Man One. I don't know; whoever it is. They don't mean anything, but—they just—they don't know what they're doing.

Man Two. But who is they? What is going on?

MAN ONE. The bench'll protect us. You ready? Just stand behind me and shut up. Here he comes. (*A person enters from offstage left, runs across stage, and leaps into the offstage right wing which is the abyss also. We hear a long yell echoing like someone falling.* MAN ONE *and* MAN TWO *watch.*)

MAN TWO. (MAN TWO *over to offstage right looking over into abyss.*) Oh my God.

MAN ONE. Don't say that. Hey fella? Fella?

MAN TWO. What?

MAN ONE. I don't want to hear that. You understand?

MAN TWO. Hear what?

MAN ONE. God. Don't say God. I don't want to hear that. You understand me?

MAN TWO. Why not?

MAN ONE. I just don't want to talk about it all right. You want to be friends, okay, but that's a condition. You understand?

MAN TWO. All right, all right. If it bothers you. I . . . I won't say it.

MAN ONE. Thank you. (MAN ONE *turns bench around, sits.*)

MAN TWO. (MAN TWO *at abyss.*) He . . . uh . . . just right in?

MAN ONE. What?

MAN TWO. I said, he just went . . . ran right . . . jumped.

MAN ONE. A lot of them like that.

MAN TWO. There are?

MAN ONE. Oh yea.

MAN TWO. You see a lot of them?

MAN ONE. Stick around.

MAN TWO. Just right . . . (*Motions down to abyss.*)

MAN ONE. Right off. What do you expect, it's the edge. That's what happens.

MAN TWO. Uh huh.

MAN ONE. Oh you'd be surprised. Some of the least likely people you'd ever suspect. People that seemed . . . seemed never to ever even give it a glance. Soon . . . (*Whistles down a scale while giving hand motion down.*)

MAN TWO. (*Slow nod yes.*) I had a friend who . . . (*Does whistle and motion. Over to downstage right.*)

MAN ONE. Good friend?

MAN TWO. Kind of . . . yea. Kind of a good friend. I knew him a long time. I used to work with him. Shocked everybody.

MAN ONE. I used to be surprised. I'm used to it.

MAN TWO. Good father, good job—insurance company. Nice wife: A little demanding but comforting. Three children: all in high school. Fine house, two cars, vacations—seemed like he was enjoying it all. One day . . . (*Does whistle and motion.*)

MAN ONE. (*Nods yes.*)

MAN TWO. And there's a lot like that? Like the fellow just now?

MAN ONE. (*Nods yes.*) Bullets.

MAN TWO. What?

MAN ONE. That's what I call 'em: Bullets. They're like bullets—fast, quick. Here, there, gone.

MAN TWO. Bullets.

MAN ONE. (*Nods yes.*) That's what I call them. You have to watch out for them though, they hurt a lot of people.

MAN TWO. I guess they could.

MAN ONE. Hell, I've seen them carry children with them right off. Children yelling. (*Does whistle and motion.*) Right off.

MAN TWO. (*Looks over edge, shakes head.*)

MAN ONE. I saw one guy — he had a girl about nine on his back, two small children in his arm, and he was dragging his wife with his right hand. Dragging her. Fighting all the way. All the way to the edge. And he got them all over. All four of them. That's the most I've ever seen anyone take at once: four. But that's a bullet. Quick, one track mind, decision, right over. But there's no courage in that. That's quick impulse, no challenge. I like to see a challenge.

MAN TWO. You mean a fight, on the edge?

MAN ONE. Well, not a fight between two people. A fight with one person, between him and himself. A challenge, conflict. A "should I, shouldn't I, yes, no". Like in plays, movies. You know what I mean, that nobleness of the well thought out decision — the Heroic Dive!

MAN TWO. (*Looking at abyss.*) A heroic dive.

MAN ONE. Yea, a calm, noble, heroic dive into the abyss. And I've seen it.

MAN TWO. You have?

MAN ONE. Sure, I've seen it. There was a priest here last week. For three months he was preening, preparing, debating. It's dramatic to watch.

MAN TWO. And you watched him?

MAN ONE. I wouldn't miss something like that for the world. It was one of the best preparations I've ever seen, too. He didn't believe in his, what did he call it, "a magic show," that's what he called it. He would always come drunk, staggering around, crawling to the edge, yelling obscenties into the abyss. He did. And he loved it. He used to lay there on his stomach, hanging over the edge, screaming, laughing. He used to get some sort of deep satisfaction out of it too.

MAN TWO. Did you talk to him at all?

MAN ONE. No, I just watched. He used to come real drunk, sober up, and he'd go back, come real drunk, sober up, and go back. Then he started coming sober, lecturing to himself on walking the abyss. He even has a book of poetry he wrote here. It's published. It's called, *Walking The Abyss.*

MAN TWO. And he finally . . . (*Does whistle and motion.*)

MAN ONE. Yup.

MAN TWO. A priest?

MAN ONE. Yup. Why does that surprise you?

MAN TWO. Yea, a priest. Well, I always thought—I mean—a priest.

MAN ONE. The day before Christmas he went.

MAN TWO. No.

MAN ONE. Don't believe me?

MAN TWO. Oh, I believe you. I just—I mean—a priest.

MAN ONE. There's a lot of bullets around Christmas time. It's the holidays; brings out the loneliness.

MAN. TWO. (*Looking into abyss.*) The edge of the abyss.

MAN ONE. Well, actually, the priest didn't jump. He was going to jump; he was preening. I know he was going to jump.

MAN TWO. The edge.

MAN ONE. But strangely enough he . . . he started trying to stop a lot of others. And he did. He stopped quite a few bullets. Some would sneak back at night when he wasn't around and (*Does whistle and motion.*) But he stopped quite a few of them. I remember one guy he stopped twice.

MAN TWO. Nothing. To be nothing.

MAN ONE. He wasn't that strong either. He was big,

but fat. He was pretty fat. Broke my bench twice he did. (*Laughs.*) Not sitting on it, no. You know what he used to do? Fella? Hey fella?

MAN TWO. What?

MAN ONE. You know what he used to do?

MAN TWO. Who?

MAN ONE. The priest. The fat priest.

MAN TWO. No. (*Looks back to abyss.*) What did he do?

MAN ONE. (*Laughs.*) He used to throw my bench in front of them. He would stand up, listen to where they're coming from, pick up the bench, wait till he could see them coming, and then he'd run out, (*Laughs.*) and he used to throw my bench in front of them. Broke a lot of legs he did, a lot of 'em. Broke my bench twice. Then one day one bullet took him with him. Dragged him right over. He would've jumped anyway. I mean, eventually he would have. It's hard to hang out here without jumping.

MAN TWO. (*On stomach yelling in abyss.*) Hello. (*Echoes.*) Hello. (*Echoes.*)

MAN ONE. One guy came every week or two and he used to throw a young girl in and leave. It looked like he thought about jumping in, but he never did. And every week or two he'd come, throw a girl in, and leave. And the next week, another one and another one. Always young girls too.

MAN TWO. Hello. (*Echoes.*)

MAN ONE. I was going to report him but . . . but I figured . . . you know it was . . . it was none of my business. I don't want to get involved with anything back there. You know what I mean? Hey fella? Hey fella?

Man Two. (*Turns.*) What?

Man One. You know what I mean? I don't want to get involved.

Man Two. Yea. Yea, I know what you mean. (*Back to abyss.*)

Man One. Well, anyway, some people came one day and' they threw him over. He must have thrown ten, eleven, women over before they threw him over. Hanging around here you see a lot of strangeness. It's sacred here, it's more intense. (*Points to head.*) More activity up here.

Man Two. (*Yelling into abyss.*) I can't take it. *I Can't Take It!*

Man One. Something about this place that tends to draw the dramatic. That's why it's easy to sit here, there's always something. (*Opens small bag at his feet, takes out newspaper.*) Let's see what's in the news today.

Man Two. (*Yelling into abyss.*) Life Sucks!

Man One. That's not new. People thought of that hundreds of thousands of years ago.

Man Two. (*Into abyss.*) You're not getting no Goddamn divorce money from me.

Man One. "The Dow Jones industrial average closed up a point"—whatever that means.

Man Two. (*Into abyss.*) You hear me?

Man One. Here's one: "Taxi collides with train killing three instantly." That looks interesting. Page Nine.

Man Two. (*Into abyss.*) No alimony for you.

Man One. (*Turning pages.*) Six, seven . . . here it is.

Man Two. (*Into abyss.*) You ain't getting *nothing* from me, Mary!

Man One. "They were racing to get across the rail

tracks when they saw the lights blinking." Wow. Listen to this.

MAN TWO. You hear me, Mary!

MAN ONE. "The taxi was dragged a quarter of a mile before the train could be stopped." Dragged. Imagine that—dragged a quarter of a mile.

MAN TWO. (*Into abyss.*) You hear me! Nothing! You ain't getting nothing.

MAN ONE. What a drag. (*Laughs.*) Get it fella? What a drag? (*Laughs.*)

MAN TWO. (*Into the abyss.*) I hate computers.

MAN ONE. No sense of humor. That's one thing around here, there's no sense of humor.

MAN TWO. Goddamn computers. Goddamn data processing crap!

MAN ONE. Let's see what else is new. (*Into newspaper.*) Oh here's one: "Terrorists gun down three in skyjacking." Page eighteen. (*Turning pages.*) Sixteen, seventeen—what the hell—there's no page eighteen.

MAN TWO. Life Sucks!

MAN ONE. They forgot page eighteen. I can see the comics, but . . .

MAN TWO. Life Sucks!

MAN ONE. (*To* MAN TWO.) Having fun? Fella? Hey Fella?

MAN TWO. (*Sits up from hanging over abyss.*) Yea? Did you want me?

MAN ONE. Having fun?

MAN TWO. (*Smiles and shrugs.*)

MAN ONE. It has a nice echo, doesn't it?

MAN TWO. Yea.

MAN ONE. It rings and rings.

MAN TWO. (*Snickers.*) It does.

MAN ONE. Nice sound, isn't it?

MAN TWO. Yea, I guess.

MAN ONE. Clear, very clear sound. That's one of the nicest sounds to yell, too.

MAN TWO. What is?

MAN ONE. Life sucks. The "Sucks" with the hard "K"? It's clear. It bounces well. (*Imitates the echo.*) Sucks! Doesn't it? Doesn't it tend to ring well?

MAN TWO. I guess.

MAN ONE. I like that sound. That's a popular one too. "Life sucks." Real popular. The real popular ones are: "Life sucks"; it used to be "Life stinks", but now the "sucks" took over. And, uh . . . let's see, "Life sucks." "I can't take it," and "I can't take it anymore." The same one, I guess, depending on whether you like to have "anymore" on the end or not. What else do I hear?

MAN TWO. It almost seems to talk back.

MAN ONE. What?

MAN TWO. I said: It almost seems to talk back; the echoes.

MAN ONE. Yes, it does, doesn't it.

MAN TWO. Yea.

MAN ONE. Yea, that's why I like it. It's honest. Whatever you say, it agrees with you.

MAN TWO. (*Into abyss.*) Hello!

MAN ONE. It's honest. What you give it, it gives you.

MAN TWO. (*Into abyss.*) Hello!

MAN ONE. Not like life. (*Over to abyss, hanging over with him, but just barely. The cord won't let him get that close.*) You're honest aren't you? Aren't you?

MAN TWO. I should.

MAN ONE. You're frightening you're so honest.

MAN TWO. Who cares?

MAN ONE. No games.

MAN TWO. Who cares?

MAN ONE. Just a pure nothing devouring. (MAN TWO *stands, walks up to* MAN ONE. MAN ONE *stands and draws back.* MAN TWO *extends hand for handshake.*)

MAN TWO. Uh . . . Thank you for saying hello. It was nice talking to you. Nice meeting you.

MAN ONE. Well, it was nice meeting you. (*They shake.*) What was your name?

MAN TWO. Uh . . . well, I'd rather not say.

MAN ONE. Then don't . . . don't. I'll call you . . . Number Two. That's what I'll call you—Number Two. How's that?

MAN TWO. Okay.

MAN ONE. I'm Number One.

MAN TWO. Allright, then, nice meeting you, Number One.

MAN ONE. (*They shake again.*) Nice meeting you, Number Two. I get the impression you're leaving.

MAN TWO. (*Nods yes.*) Yea, I'm going to (*Does whistle down.*) Now. (*Walks to downstage right.*)

MAN ONE. Oh good for you. You've made a decision?

MAN TWO. (*Nods yes.*)

MAN ONE. It takes courage.

MAN TWO. I guess.

MAN ONE. And you've thought about it?

MAN TWO. Yea.

MAN ONE. You're ready to accept the responsibility for your own actions and all that existential crap?

MAN TWO. Yea. I think so.

MAN ONE. Well, then you're ready for the big whistle. (*Does whistle.*)

MAN TWO. The big whistle. I guess I'm as ready as I'll ever be.

MAN ONE. Courage. The Heroic Dive. Good for you. I'm proud of you, you know. I'm proud.

MAN TWO. You are?

MAN ONE. Sure I am. This takes courage. It does — a lot of it.

MAN TWO. When you saw me, Number One, did you think I was going to?

MAN ONE. The only thing I know about people is you never know about them. How's that for a slogan?

MAN TWO. Yea, but . . . but what did you think?

MAN ONE. I don't. I've tried to stop. Remember what I said before?

MAN TWO. Oh. That's right.

MAN ONE. But it didn't seem like you were.

MAN TWO. Oh no?

MAN ONE. No. No, I figured you yelled, got it a bit out of your system. Lots of people do that you know. Come here, yell, go back. I never see them again. I thought you might take that road.

MAN TWO. I wish I could, but I have too many reasons.

MAN ONE. Well, that's what you need.

MAN TWO. Yea . . . yea, I guess.

MAN ONE. Well good, good for you. That's good. If you're going to make a decision like this, it's . . . it's good to make it like a man. Dive like a man: head straight, back arched, chin up, and in. (*Does whistle.*)

MAN TWO. People think it's cowardly. I've always heard that.

MAN ONE. It's not. It's not cowardly.

MAN TWO. I guess it can be.

MAN ONE. Of course it can be. The bullets you know, they're cowards, they never think. But not you. I'll never

say you're a coward, whoever you are. (*Claps hands.*)
Well, then . . . if you're ready, let's see it.

MAN TWO. (*Pause.*) My wife's been cheating.

MAN ONE. What?

MAN TWO. My wife—she's been cheating.

MAN ONE. Oh.

MAN TWO. I, uh . . . I caught her.

MAN ONE. Uh huh.

MAN TWO. Yea, I told her I was going away for the weekend on business. She sent the kids away. We have two boys, four and six.

MAN ONE. (*Nods head.*)

MAN TWO. She sent the kids to her best friend's, and I never was going away on business, I just said that. I snuck back into the house about 2 a.m. . . . and there was a nice meal, all finished, candles burnt down on the dining room table, an empty wine bottle, and upstairs, uh . . . I walked up there and I opened the door to our bedroom, and she was . . . my wife that is. She was, you know, in there with this guy.

MAN ONE. (*Nods head.*)

MAN TWO. A friend. He was best man at our wedding. They went to college together, took art classes together at night twice a week. (*Shrugs shoulders.*) I don't know.

MAN ONE. The best man at your wedding? That's worth jumping for!

MAN TWO. I don't know.

MAN ONE. Sure. How long have they been doing this?

MAN TWO. Two years I found out.

MAN ONE. Two years?

MAN TWO. Yea.

MAN ONE. They've been doing this for two years?

MAN TWO. (*Nods yes.*)

MAN ONE. Behind your back?

MAN TWO. Yea.

MAN ONE. Boy, you must have really felt stupid, huh?

MAN TWO. I . . . suspected but.

MAN ONE. Two years! Wow. Your best friend and your wife. For two years. Was he a good friend?

MAN TWO. Yea. I thought so. I guess not.

MAN ONE. Wow. Did you ever tell him problems you were having in your marriage?

MAN TWO. (*Nods yes.*) Yea.

MAN ONE. Really?

MAN TWO. Sometimes.

MAN ONE. Wow! They were probably laughing it up over each one you told them.

MAN TWO. (*Looks to abyss.*) Yea I bet they were.

MAN ONE. He probably told her everything, every little gripe and problem you had. And that probably brought *them* closer.

MAN TWO. (*While looking at abyss.*) You know what they did when I opened the bedroom door and they saw me standing there watching them in bed? They both got up, got dressed, and walked past me and went to a motel.

MAN ONE. They did?

MAN TWO. Yea. (*Nods head.*)

MAN ONE. They walked right past you and went to a motel?

MAN TWO. (*Nods yes.*)

MAN ONE. How do you know they went to a motel?

MAN TWO. She said, "Let's go to a motel," and they walked past me.

MAN ONE. Now that's courage! That takes guts. Ah, forget it, your marriage is over.

MAN TWO. Yea.

MAN ONE. And to think, you even paid for the art classes, the wine, the bed springs. (*Snickers.*) She probably even chipped in your money—your hard earned money—for half the motel.

MAN TWO. I shouldn't of snuck home. I knew it. I knew he was up there. I knew it.

MAN ONE. You catch 'em doing it?

MAN TWO. No, they were in bed. They were just laying there, hugging, kissing. But I knew it.

MAN ONE. Did they have the covers over them? They might have been.

MAN TWO. No, they weren't.

MAN ONE. They probably just got finished. Yea, that's worth jumping for.

MAN TWO. I don't know. If I give up I'm just giving them the whole thing. You know?

MAN ONE. Ah, they get the whole thing anyway. You might as well bail out. Wow, two years.

MAN TWO. But *I* caught her. How can *she* tell me she wants a divorce?

MAN ONE. She'll lie. For the house and car, and money, and furniture, and *china?* Ah, they lie like hell.

MAN TWO. How can she lie? I caught her. In bed. Right there.

MAN ONE. You have any witnesses?

MAN TWO. (*Shrugs.*) Him.

MAN ONE. And he's going to admit it? Testify on your behalf against her that he was in bed with your wife? Wrong. No witnesses, she'll counter suit, dig up some stuff on you. Like, uh . . . you drink?

MAN TWO. Yea, I do.

MAN ONE. A lot? You drink a lot?

MAN TWO. Yea, lately I have been.

MAN ONE. How "Lately?"

MAN TWO. Uh . . . the last year or so kind of a lot. Business hasn't been doing to good either. (*Looking into abyss.*)

MAN ONE. There you go. Unfit: you lose. No children, no home, no furniture. You might get a car though. Oh, that's right. I forgot to tell you: some people come in cars! You really have to watch out for them. It's best to hide behind a tree. They go right off with the cars too. (*Imitates car sound with horn, brakes, going over edge.*) Right off. Some of them doing a hundred, a hundred-twenty miles an hour. A lot of young kids too. Four wheels up in the air, twirling around end over end. At night it's pretty interesting to watch, cause the head lights flash in all different directions when they go down.

MAN TWO. You think I should jump?

MAN ONE. No, you won't jump. You were never going to. You're too scared.

MAN TWO. I'm not scared. I . . . I just.

MAN ONE. Sure you are. You're scared.

MAN TWO. No, I'm not, I'm just . . . I don't know what to do.

MAN ONE. You're scared.

MAN TWO. (*To abyss.*) I don't even know what to think. I mean did you ever think that there is no meaning to why life is? That life just *is*, and when—when we die, we just die, and that's it, there's no reason to all this. It's just an absurd, stupid happening in nature and—and we happen to be unfortunate enough to think, and know, and be conscious of how stupid it all is that we exist.

MAN ONE. I told you, I stopped thinking as much as possible. I just watch. It's healthier that way.

MAN TWO. I work for a company. In systems. We program computers. I hate it. Everyday I hate it. When

I get up, I walk to our bathroom, look in the mirror, toothbrush in one hand, toothpaste in the other, and I squint, and look at my blur and I say, "How come I'm not happy? I work so hard. How come I can't do what I want? Life is short. How come I'm not happy?" Then I go to work, I get off work, I eat, I watch T.V., I wake up and there's the mirror again, there's the blur, there's the questions. I've worked so hard for just that blur. And now I'm losing it all. *I'm Losing It All.*

MAN ONE. It's peaceful in there number two. Go for it.

MAN TWO. (*To abyss.*) But my two kids. I have two kids to look out for.

MAN ONE. I do have one link back there though. I get the newspaper.

MAN TWO. Those poor kids. They don't know anything.

MAN ONE. You know why I get the paper. (*Picks up paper.*) Because they always have stories on who went off the day before, where they lived, the notes they left, how they did it, a little summary of why. They try to dig right to the marrow of how desperate they really were. (*Pointing to newspaper.*) Now I saw this yesterday.

MAN TWO. (*Looking into the abyss.*) My children.

MAN ONE. (*Reads from paper.*) "Tom Lonny, 26, and Frieda Dekleck, 21, of Two Town Road, Phonic Township, were found in Tom Lonny's garage with his automobile running and a vacuum cleaner hose attached to the exhaust pipe entering the back right rear window. Frieda Dekleck was bound by her hands and feet in the back seat, and her boy friend, Tom Lonny, was found in the front seat."

MAN TWO. Who takes care of the children if we give up?

MAN ONE. Oh, this is interesting. (*Reading again.*)

"A suicide note written in Mr. Lonny's handwriting found on the dash board of the automobile read quote, 'If I can't have her, no one can,' unquote. The two were pronounced dead on arrival at Memorial Hospital." (*Puts down the paper.*) Dramatic huh? I saw them yesterday.

MAN TWO. The poor children.

MAN ONE. Look here's a picture. Geez . . . look at that. Here's how he ran the hose into the car.

MAN TWO. (*Turns to* MAN ONE.) You know something? So what if my wife wins the case? So what? Right number one?

MAN ONE. What?

MAN TWO. I said, so what if my wife wins the case, gets the divorce? So what?

MAN ONE. So then she gets all your belongings.

MAN TWO. So what?

MAN ONE. You like your belongings?

MAN TWO. That might be better. I can start over. I'll be single again.

MAN ONE. You pay alimony.

MAN TWO. So I pay alimony. So she gets the house, the car, so what? I could date. I could get another job. I could do what I want. I could be free.

MAN ONE. No one's free.

MAN TWO. I *would* be free.

MAN ONE. No such thing.

MAN TWO. I'll get my own apartment, my own car. I could actually get another occupation. I'd go where I want, when I want.

MAN ONE. And I thought this was going to be easy for you.

MAN TWO. It will be easy. I can start over.

MAN ONE. No, I'm talking about going in, diving. It's going to be a long process for you, buddy.

MAN TWO. Why'd you say that?

MAN ONE. It's going to take time. You're going to become a regular before you go in. I feel sorry for you.

MAN TWO. But I just said I made up my mind I'm *not* going in.

MAN ONE. There's going to be a lot of questions and long nights. There's going to be a lot of pain. I feel sorry for you.

MAN TWO. What are you telling me that for? Why are you saying this?

MAN ONE. I'm just telling you from my experiences being here what I think.

MAN TWO. But I just told you I'm not going in, so what are you saying that for?

MAN ONE. I'm just saying it.

MAN TWO. Why? How come? Because you know it seems to me that you're trying to prod me to jump.

MAN ONE. I don't prod people to jump.

MAN TWO. It seems it.

MAN ONE. I'm telling the truth. I'm telling you what I see.

MAN TWO. In fact, it seems to me you're kind of anxious to see anybody go in.

MAN ONE. Well, that's a hell of an accusation. What, do you think I enjoy it?

MAN TWO. Well, watching you it seems you kinda' do. Yea, I'd say you enjoy it.

MAN ONE. I find it interesting.

MAN TWO. You almost seem to feed on it.

MAN ONE. Oh, come on now.

MAN TWO. Your stories, your newspapers, your dramatic verbal gymnastics of disasters you've stared at. It almost seems you get some sort of strength from it.

MAN ONE. That's ridiculous.

MAN TWO. I mean, your face lights up everytime a

bullet flies by. Why? How come? What are you doing here watching all this?

MAN ONE. And what else am I going to do but watch? I don't like to watch. But when I watch I don't have to think. So I watch, time flies by, I don't have to think, and I enjoy that. I do. That's why I watch. But what else can I do? Give me another alternative.

MAN TWO. Why don't you jump? If you jump you don't have to do either.

MAN ONE. Oh, now look *who's* prodding *who* to jump.

MAN TWO. I'm not prodding anybody.

MAN ONE. Now you sound like me.

MAN TWO. But you said you wanted to jump. You just said it. So why not? I mean if you want to, why not? I'll cheer for you.

MAN ONE. I told you why.

MAN TWO. You told me you were in a hospital bed with some wires and a nurse. But where's the problem? You can jump.

MAN ONE. It's not like that. I can't; it's not that simple.

MAN TWO. Why isn't it simple? It's there, you're here: jump!

MAN ONE. I can't; you can, bullets can. That's why I sit here, why I want to see someone make the decision, make the dive. I can't.

MAN TWO. You can't decide.

MAN ONE. Oh no. If I could I would.

MAN TWO. You would?

MAN ONE. Yes.

MAN TWO. You would like to?

MAN ONE. I'd love to. It's impossible. I can't go any further than the edge.

MAN TWO. Of course you can. Just go for it like you tell me. Close your eyes, and run across the edge.

MAN ONE. You don't understand.

MAN TWO. Just do it.

MAN ONE. All right. You see this cord here you asked me about?

MAN TWO. Yea.

MAN ONE. It's tied to me.

MAN TWO. I know. I figured that out.

MAN ONE. I can't take it off. It's attached.

MAN TWO. To the hospital.

MAN ONE. That's right. It's attached to the hospital. And I can only go to the edge. That's all. That's how far it reaches. I can't go over, they won't let me.

MAN TWO. The hospital won't?

MAN ONE. That's right. I would've went over if they didn't put this cord on but—but that's life.

MAN TWO. Then cut the cord.

MAN ONE. I can't cut the cord.

MAN TWO. Why not?

MAN ONE. I don't want to talk about it.

MAN TWO. Just answer me that: Why can't you cut it?

MAN ONE. Because I'm not strong enough. I'm not physically able to cut it. And they know it.

MAN TWO. But if you could, you would.

MAN ONE. If I could? Yea. Oh Yea. And you know how I'd go if I could? I'd go in one of those cars around one hundred and twenty miles an hour, floored to the floor, with the high beams on. That's how I'd go. Yea, and on some real clear dark moonless night I'd go. It's quite a show with the lights flashing. Or maybe just two lights, a flashlight in each hand, and I'd just dive down screaming. (MAN TWO *stands, walks behind the bench.*)

MAN TWO. Number One, if you want to cut the cord

that bad, you want to go over, if you're that stuck, (MAN TWO *picks up cord.*) I'll cut it. I'll cut it for you.

MAN ONE. (*Stands.*) NO! Put it down.

MAN TWO. If you can't like you say, I'll do it.

MAN ONE. No. I . . . I don't want to right now. (MAN ONE goes over and grabs cord also.)

MAN TWO. I can, and you can go.

MAN ONE. No. No you better not.

MAN TWO. I can do it. It's simple.

MAN ONE. You can't do that for someone else. You'll be an accomplice for my going over the edge. I don't want that.

MAN TWO. So I'll be an accomplice. So what?

MAN ONE. So you'll get in trouble. You'll be arrested by the police.

MAN TWO. I don't care. You ready?

MAN ONE. You'll be arrested.

MAN TWO. I said: I don't care. (*Looking at cord.*) I can tear this, no problem. One quick tear, you'll be in. Ready?

MAN ONE. Put it down.

MAN TWO. This is your chance Number One.

MAN ONE. (*Intense.*) Could you please put that down.

MAN TWO. You're going to throw away your big chance. You can go over in one rip.

MAN ONE. Could you please *put that down.*

MAN TWO. This is sturdy but I can do it.

MAN ONE. I'm not getting you in trouble.

MAN TWO. Don't worry about me, think about you. This your moment.

MAN ONE. Put the wire down.

MAN TWO. Say yes.

MAN ONE. Put the wire down!

Man Two. Say yes. Yes, I'm ready for the abyss. Head up, chin out, back arched, and dive.

Man One. PUT THAT DAMN WIRE DOWN! (Man Two *drops wire.*) What the hell's wrong with you? (*Sits down.*) Can't you see I don't want to dive?

Man Two. But you said you wanted to.

Man One. So what.

Man Two. I thought you just didn't want to get me in trouble and if I kept asking.

Man One. I don't want to. I *don't want* to. I never want to. (*Turns to* Man Two.) Because I'm alive.

Man Two. That's why?

Man One. Yes.

Man Two. Because you're alive.

Man One. That's why.

Man Two. But why be alive like this?

Man One. (*Shrugs.*) Why not? I don't have anything anywhere, but I'm alive. That's something ain't it: Life. Ain't it?

Man Two. I guess.

Man One. I might not like to think about it, but I've got it. And I'm not giving it up. I, uh, I had this choice before to cut the wire, even legally I've had it. I don't want to. When it comes down to the moment of cutting the cord, I never do.

Man Two. You don't want to go back there, you don't want to go in there, you just want to stay here?

Man One. I can't fit in back there, don't want to fit in over there, so I'm stuck, on the edge.

Man Two. I see.

Man One. For life.

Man Two. I'm sorry. And I'm sorry I was pushing you.

MAN ONE. I guess I brought that on myself. You know I was trying to get you to dive. Sometimes I think I try to convince myself that that's the noble think to do.

MAN TWO. I, uh . . . I'm going to get going. I'm going to go back. I know where there's a real nice apartment for rent; I'm going to go look at it.

MAN ONE. Good for you. That takes more courage than those idiots. Good for you Number Two. They make it look so easy and simple going over the edge. Depending how you use it I guess, thought is our salvation and our damnation.

MAN TWO. Number one. (*Extends hand to shake.*) Nice meeting you.

MAN ONE. Yea. (*They shake.*) Maybe we'll meet again sometime.

MAN TWO. No. No, I doubt that.

MAN ONE. Good for you again then. (*Stands, looks upstage left.*) Listen? Hear that?

MAN TWO. (*Points upstage left.*) It's coming from over there.

MAN ONE. Yea. (*Turns bench around.*)

MAN TWO. I'm going that way. (*Points upstage center.*)

MAN ONE. Okay. He's coming fast.

MAN TWO. He is. Bye one.

MAN ONE. Goodbye two. (MAN TWO *exits upstage center.*) Goodbye. (*We hear a man groan from upstage left.*) Come on idiot. Let's see a good one. Come on baby. (*We hear footsteps, a man enters offstage left running, screaming across stage, and exits offstage right: Going over edge.*) (MAN ONE *walks over and looks into offstage right.*) Lucky bastard. (MAN ONE *turns, goes back to bench, sits, and puts head in hands.*) (*Lights fade.*) (*Curtain.*)

PROPERTY LIST

A bench
A newspaper in a small bag
An extension cord (red)

COSTUMES

MAN ONE: all in white
MAN TWO: blue three piece suit (red tie)

SCENE DESIGN: A BENCH AT THE EDGE

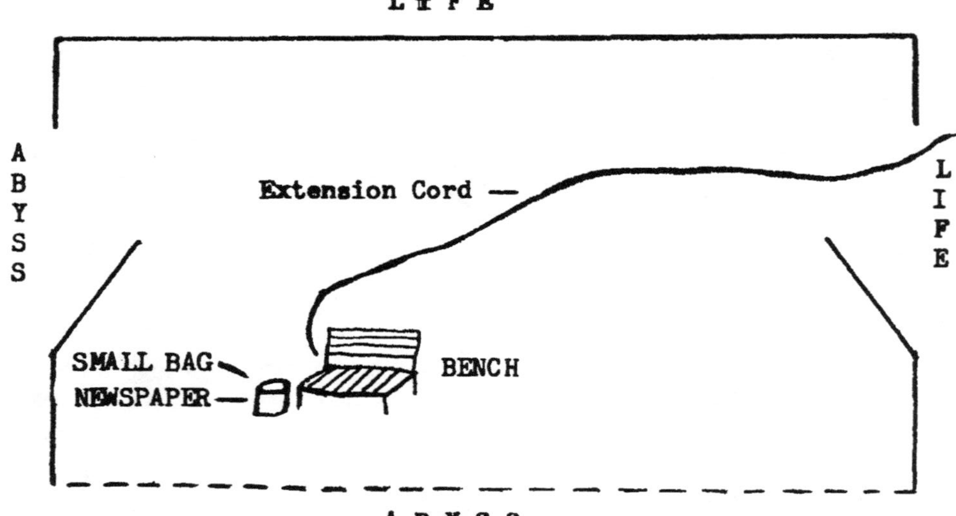

Period

SET: *A modern kitchen in contemporary England. It looks lived in. There is a table, some chairs, the usual bits and pieces: A sink, a stove and so on. The table is half set for breakfast.*

CHARACTERS

Janet Matthews
Harry Matthews
The Gasman

Period

(Lights up to reveal JANET *sitting at the table fiddling with the butter dish, while* HARRY *is looking round the room for his shoes. It is early morning, the light is harsh, flourescent)*

HARRY. Where are my shoes?

JANET. Where you left them.

HARRY. That's stupid, you know, that's really stupid. Of course they're where I left them, where else could they be? The whole point is I can't remember where that is.

JANET. I could have moved them.

HARRY. Have you been moving my shoes?

JANET. No . . . but I could have done.

HARRY. Will you kindly shut up and just tell me where my shoes are?

JANET. Where you left them.

HARRY. Janet!

JANET. Well how the hell am I supposed to know where they are? Am I my husband's shoes' keeper?

HARRY. Probably.

JANET. Toast?

HARRY. What?

JANET. I said: Toast? It's an abbreviated form of the longer sentence: would you like to eat some toast this morning, light of my life. Toast?

HARRY. *(Still looking for shoes.)* Mmmm, okay, toast.

JANET. Fine, toast. Meaning, yes, fire of my loins, I would like you to place some of that doughy substance known as bread under the dancing blue flames of the grill until all the white particles have been burnt or oxidised into brown ones, thus producing what is, in common parlance, known as toast.

HARRY. What are you rambling on about now?

JANET. Subtext, my dear, that is all, just the subtext.

HARRY. Never mind the subtext, where are my shoes?

JANET. In the bathroom, by the scales.

HARRY. Thank *you*. Now perhaps I can get on. Heaven knows what they're doing up there. . . . (HARRY *exits:* JANET *prepares breakfast.*)

JANET. (*Picks up salt.*) Salt—of the earth. Treasured mineral, root of salary, from the latin, salarium, soldiers paid in salt. Pepper—rhymes with leper. Unclean! Unclean! (*Hobbles round like a leper.*) Milk—not to be cried over when split. Comes from cows' tits. Poor cows. (*Feels her breasts.*) Slurp slurp. Twice a day, week in week out. Five in the morning, five at night. Slurp, slurp. (HARRY *enters to see* JANET *squeezing breasts.*)

HARRY. What are you doing?

JANET. Being a cow.

HARRY. My shoes weren't there.

JANET. I told you I didn't know where they were.

HARRY. Oh, yes, very funny, very funny I'm sure. Send your husband on a fool's errand time, is it? Oh most amusing. Let's bait hubby, shall we, see how late we can make him for work.

JANET. Sarcasm—not *necessarily* the lowest form of wit . . . Cereal?

HARRY. What?

JANET. Cereal, meaning . . .

HARRY. Okay, okay, yes. God, what a mess.

JANET. Are you referring to the cereal, the kitchen, me, or life in general?

HARRY. Have the papers arrived?

JANET. Have the papers arrived. Telepathy never was my strong point, but I would say that since it isn't yet eight they probably, in all likelyhood, assuming that to-day will not differ from the last thousand odd, have not. But don't trust me—statistical probability is renowned for its inaccuracy. Go and take a look.

HARRY. This is incredible.

JANET. You like the cereal? I'm so glad. It's the same one we've been having for the past ten years, ever since your mother suggested you needed more ruffage. Exciting, isn't it? I mean don't you lie in bed each morning and think, after you've coughed and lit a cigarette and slobbered over me, I mean, don't you lie back, stare up at the ceiling, and think to yourself, with that warm feeling inside, that in half an hour or so I'll be munching through a whole bowl of delicious All Bran. The crisp flakes, the crunchy granules of sugar, the cool creaminess of the milk—it's enough to make your saliva thicken! Then you generally roll over, fart, and go to the bathroom before I can make it round the bed. Ah, life's little pleasures!

HARRY. Janet?

JANET. Yes, my ferocious lover?

HARRY. The toast's burning.

JANET. Oh no! The toast's burning! My God, what shall we do? Jesus Christ, the toast's burning! The Matthews are having a blissful breakfast and the toast's burning. What are they going to do? Will they ring for the fire brigade? Will they douse the stove in buckets of water? Will they make passionate love on the kitchen table in an attempt to grasp one final moment of ecstasy before they are consummed in toast-engulfing flames? What will happen? Will they ever have breakfast again? Can life as we know it go on?

HARRY. (*Rescuing toast.*) I don't know what's wrong

with you this morning.

JANET. Your mother likes burnt toast.

HARRY. What has that got to do with it?

JANET. Well, it just proves that taste in toast is not hereditary. Strange how common experience can add to the body of scientific knowledge, isn't it?

HARRY. I wish the papers would arrive.

JANET. I mean plop fell the apple, and old Newton thought to himself, funny, funny, something's up here, and what goes up must come down—and there you have it.

HARRY. Is there any tea?

JANET. Do you realise that your wife's thought patterns are disturbingly similar to Sir Isaac Newton's? Oh, many's the time I've seen an apple drop and thought to myself, my God, that means that gravity is in inverse proportion to the square root of the distance between two objects.

HARRY. You did it again. You did it again! How do you expect tea to come out if you don't put tealeaves in? Every day, it's the same every day—you put boiling water in the pot and you expect tea to come out. Who do you think you are, Christ?

JANET. I've only done it twice before. Besides, geniuses are supposed to be absent-minded.

HARRY. But you're not absent minded, you just forget to put in the tea!

JANET. So I am a genius?

HARRY. Where are the tea bags?

JANET. You mean you live here too?

HARRY. Janet, I can't take much more of this, just tell me where they are.

JANET. Oh, I'm sorry, my darling, my little flower, my lambchop, my honeypie, my little cabbage, honeydew, poochy-face, my. . . .

HARRY. Christ almighty!

JANET. What is it, have you burnt yourself?

HARRY. Burnt myself? Burnt myself! How the hell could I burn myself when I'm nowhere near the stove?

JANET. I don't know, but why else would you cry out like that? It's one thing to shout out "Ow" or even "Yikes", but it's quite another to take the Lord's name in vain. It's a serious business, you could burn for evermore if you go on like that. How would you like it if you had been nailed to a piece of wood for everybody else's sins and all the thanks you got was to have your name shouted out when people didn't burn themselves? Just ask yourself if it's fair, that's all. Now, that's not too much to ask, is it — peachy-pooh?

HARRY. What the hell are you talking about? Just what the hell are you talking about? Here I am trying to eat my breakfast, quietly and calmly trying to satisfy my hunger pains, before driving thirty miles through jam packed traffic, so I can work nine hours in a stuffy little office, so that my wife can sit at home idling away the day in luxury, and all she can do is accuse me of profanity! For Christ's sake, Janet . . .

JANET. Ah!

HARRY. Goddamnit woman, I shall say what I damn well please! If I want to say Christ Almighty in my own house, I shall . . .

JANET. Go on then, I dare you.

HARRY. (*Pause.*) No, no I shan't give you that satisfaction. I am going to the bathroom now, and then I shall leave for work, and I hope you will be in a more reasonable frame of mind when I return.

JANET. Why do you have to go to the bathroom?

HARRY. I need to brush my teeth.

JANET. Brush your teeth! You've done that once already.

HARRY. Well, I've eaten since then.

JANET. Christ, Harry, you've been getting up from this table at eight twenty precisely and going to the bathroom now for the last fifteen years, and do you still expect me to believe it's to brush your teeth? Do you think I'm that stupid? Do you think I haven't got a sense of smell? Do you honestly believe that my olfactory lobe is out of order? Do you think that after all these years I don't know what you're up to in there? Why can't you be honest for once and tell me that you're going to open you bowels, that you're taking a crap, shitting a brick, dropping your guts. It wouldn't be the end of the world to admit your excretary functions to your own wife.

HARRY. (*Pause.*) I'm going to brush my teeth. (HARRY *exits.* JANET *picks up the teapot and very deliberately drops it on the floor. She picks up the cereal packet and reads.*)

JANET. Four ounces of All Bran, two eggs well beaten, two ounces of granulated sugar, a tablespoon of butter, three ounces of chopped liver, six sheeps eyes, one aborted baby, a dead puppy . . . (*The door bell rings.*) Ah, the bell. (*Shouts to* HARRY.) There's someone at the door. Shall I tell them you're brushing your teeth? (*Goes to door.*) Who is it? My husband's in the bathroom but he's not having a shit.

GASMAN. (*From without.*) It's the gasman.

JANET. The gasman?

GASMAN. Precisely, madam, the gasman. May I come in?

JANET. Well, yes, I suppose you should. (*She opens door. The* GASMAN *enters.*)

GASMAN. Morning, mam, come to read your meter.

JANET. I'm sorry?

GASMAN. I said: Morning, mam, I've come to read your meter. I'm the gasman, or as some people like to call me, the meter man, although my official title is in fact Inspector of Domestic Metering Devices, or IDDD for short. But I don't mind, afterall what does it matter to me what people call me, as long as it isn't obscene of course, or calls attention to my rather bulbous nose. . . For instance, I remember an old lady, sweet old thing she was, widowed in the 14–18 war, well she used to call me Mr Meter—well of course, that isn't my name, oh no, a long way from it, completely different letters for a start—except the A—but I didn't complain, I was Mr Meter to her. I knew what she meant, she knew what she meant, so everything went along just fine, if ya know what I mean. Mind if I read your meter, mam?

JANET. No, of course not.

GASMAN. Fine, only some people get upset, you know, they think it an invasion of their privacy or something. Can you imagine it! Think that just because the meter is on their property they own it! Well, I let them know, I let them know loud and clear that they're sadly mistaken—sadly mistaken. The meter equipment belongs to the gas company from the moment it is conceived to the moment it is melted down to join all the other disconnected meters in the big works in the sky. Yes sir, that meter belongs to the gas company wherever it might be; I don't care if it's on the moon or in Buckingham Palace, it still belongs to the company! And that's what I tell them.

JANET. Good for you.

GASMAN. Your teapot's broken.

JANET. Yes, I dropped it on the floor.

GASMAN. Do you think I could read your meter?

JANET. *Your* meter, you mean.

GASMAN. I beg your pardon?

JANET. I'll get my husband, he's just . . .

GASMAN. Brushing his teeth? you said.

JANET. I did? Oh yes! Harry, Harry, there's someone here to see you. (*Pause, no reply. Laughs nervously.*) He must be busy.

GASMAN. With his teeth.

JANET. Harry, it's the gasman. (*Pause.*) Tea? I mean, would you like to . . .

GASMAN. Thank you, I wouldn't say no.

JANET. (*Seeing teapot.*) You wouldn't? Oh, I've got plenty more of those.

HARRY. (*Off stage.*) I suppose you think this is funny. (HARRY *appears, doing up his trousers, sees* GASMAN.) As my wife no doubt told you, I've been taking a crap.

GASMAN. Ah. I'm from the gasboard.

JANET. (*Sniggers.*)

HARRY. I see.

GASMAN. I want to read your meter.

HARRY. Ah.

GASMAN. That is, it is my job to read your meter. That is what I am employed for.

HARRY. Quite. (*Pause.*) Well, go ahead. you won't be in our way. (*To Janet.*) I may be home late tonight, dearest.

JANET. Fine with me, Harry.

HARRY. Yes, well, good, then I'll be off.

JANET. Harry?

HARRY. Yes?

JANET. Shoes. You haven't got any shoes on. A small point I know, but . . .

HARRY. Hmmmmph. Right.

GASMAN. Er, excuse me, I don't want to butt in or anything, but . . .

HARRY. Yes, what is it?

GASMAN. Well, Harry, how am I supposed to read the meter if I don't know where it is?

HARRY. But it's not our meter, is it, it's yours. You put it in, you should know where it is.

GASMAN. But it's your house.

JANET. That's true.

HARRY. Feel free to look about, it can't be very far away, and I'm sure you've had plenty of experience at this sort of thing.

GASMAN. Excuse me, sir, but I am the meter reader, not the meter searcher. It is a common fallacy I admit, and by no means restricted to you, that I should crawl around on all fours sniffing out stray gas meters. Well let me tell you this, it's not on any more. I've had enough. I've had my fill stalking dislocated appliances, yes sir. I'm fed up with poking around in dingy cupboards, stumbling in damp cellars, stooping in dusty attics — I've had it up to here, and I'm not going to take it anymore! I'm a reasonable man, give me a meter and I'll read it. I'll even use me torch if I have to, but I'll be damned if I'll waste half my morning tracking down a gas meter in someone else's house just because they're too lazy to do it themselves! Now let me give you some sound advice, Harry, just you find yourself a pair of shoes and start looking round your property for my gas meter, before I take it into my head that the whole business is nothing but a bourgeois conspiracy to wear out the working classes, and decide to estimate the reading from memory!

JANET. I think you should do as he says, Harry.

HARRY. You keep out of this, Janet. If it wasn't for you I'd be well on my way by now, and in my shoes.

GASMAN. I'm waiting, sir.

HARRY. Really, this is quite ridiculous. (*Pause.*) Oh, very well, if it will make you any happier. But I warn you . . .

GASMAN. It's usually best to start off in the attic, I find sir, work your way down, you know.

HARRY. I'll be hours late, and I've a particularly heavy day. . . .

JANET. Come on, darling, it's not every day the gasman cometh. (HARRY *exits.*)

JANET. Well!

GASMAN. Well?

JANET. Well, well, well. (*Pause.*) Would you like to sit down?

GASMAN. Thank you, don't mind if I do. Takes the weight off the old legs.

JANET. Yes, I suppose it would. (*Pause.*) Can I get you anything?

GASMAN. No, thanks, nothing for me. I'll just sit here and tot up me numbers. (*Takes out book.*)

JANET. Right, fine. (JANET *starts to clear the breakfast. A longish pause.*) Been at it long, a gasman, I mean?

GASMAN. Since a boy, mam, since a boy.

JANET. Oh that's nice.

GASMAN. If you like gas.

JANET. Yes. (*Pause.*) And I suppose you do.

GASMAN. Can't say I does, can't say I doesn't.

JANET. Oh.

GASMAN. I mean gas's gas, isn't it. It's difficult to get worked up over something you can't even see.

JANET. I suppose so.

GASMAN. It's not like water. Now if you work for the Water Board you get a real feel for the job. Everybody likes water — good, clean, clear, fresh water — it's a basic necessity for life. Who needs gas?

JANET. Well, it can be very useful at times.

GASMAN. Water, on the other hand, that's primoral, isn't it? I mean water was here long before we were. Good old H2O was around in abundance before Man was even thought of, let alone thinking. There's history there, in water, you feel you sort of belong.

JANET. But there must have been gas too.

GASMAN. 70% of the human body is made up of water. How much gas do you find in your average man on the street, heh?

JANET. All the same . . .

GASMAN. Then again you can see water; you can see it, smell it, touch it, taste it, hear it — it's all there. When it leaks you can see that it leaks. You don't get blown sky high for just lighting a fag in the water works — not that is, unless there's some gas about. It's altogether a more secure job.

JANET. Then why are you a gasman?

GASMAN. Why are the trees green, why is the sky blue? Circumstance, mam, circumstance — it's the net that surrounds us all. My old man was with the board, and his dad before him.

JANET. A family tradition?

GASMAN. If you like, I'd rather call it the hand of fate. It was expected of the eldest — to work for the Board.

JANET. How splendid! And will your son follow in his father's footsteps.

GASMAN. My son? He's still at school.

JANET. But soon to enter the profession of his ancestors.

GASMAN. Not bloody likely! I'll do my damndest to keep him out.

JANET. That shouldn't be difficult.

GASMAN. No, only he's taken it into his head that all he wants to do is read other people's meters for the rest of his life. Been seeing a sight too much of his grand-father, if you ask me. Thinks all he has to do is wander around on a bicycle chatting and snuffing out lampposts.

JANET. How romantic!

GASMAN. Stupid boy! He's got to see the light some-day, the world doesn't stand still you know . . .

JANET. I think it's rather sweet. I remember the days of the gasman on his bicycle—I used to see him on my way home from school.

GASMAN. Did he offer you sweets?

JANET. No, he always scowled at me. I used to cross the road.

GASMAN. Can't have been my father, then. Nearly bankrupted the family by giving away sweets to every child he saw. It was a great relief to my mother when they put the electric lights in, for a while that is, 'cos then he took to going round the parks distributing chocolates gratis to any kid who talked to him. In the end we had to coat a whole bag in nutmeg—after that the children used to avoid him. Broke his heart, of course, but at least we had something to eat at home.

JANET. I've always wanted to be a gasman.

GASMAN. You?

JANET. Yes. I know it's strange, but ever since I was a small girl, and I was smaller than most, I've wanted to be a gasman. I suppose you could call it my ambition in life. You know, that wonderful feeling of being a small but vital cog in the vast machinery that makes up the Gas Company. How that name is music in my ears. To be involved in that wonderful enterprise of bringing so much warmth and happiness into so many homes!

GASMAN. It's not all fun and games, you know.

JANET. But can't you see the romance of it all! The sheer strength of Man as he taps the wildest forces of

Nature and brings them right here, into the womb of my house, to heat *my* kettle of water. Are you sure I can't make you some tea?

GASMAN. I feel like a peeping-tom sometimes, you know, snooping round other people's houses looking for that damned machine. Somehow it just don't feel right—it's like I've got a tag on them. If I had my way I'd stick them on the outside of the house, then I could just walk by and read them off.

JANET. Drilling down through hundreds of feet of water, cutting deep into the earth's crust with diamond bits, gnawing through thousands of years of deposits, layer after layer of primeval rock, deep into the huge fields of pure, natural gas, hidden from sight since the beginning of time! And all those beautiful pipes!

GASMAN. Better still, I'd have them mounted on the chimneys, the left handside on the right, the righthand-side on the left. Then all I would have to do would be sit in my van with a pair of binoculars and read them off.

JANET. Mile after mile of steel piping—perfectly cylindrical, perfectly sealed. Can you imagine that, mile after mile!

GASMAN. 'Course I put it in the suggestions box—but do they take any notice? Don't you believe it! (*Confidentially.*) Vested interests. That's what it is, mate, vested bloody interests. They think I'd be putting them out of a job, putting myself out of a job comes to that. But I keep telling them, someone would have to take out all the old meters, run pipes up the outside of the house, and fix the new meters on the chimneys! It would take thousands! All those houses, all those meters, all those chimneys! Chimney after chimney after chimney after chimney . . . It makes me giddy to think about it. That's all it needs, a bit of imagination, a shifting around, reorganising labour, and hey presto everybody's happy! Thousands of new jobs, no bother with that bloody gasman calling again, and I could sit nice and comfy in me van with me binocs!

JANET. That first rush of gas as the bowels of the earth release their precious treasure, up the tubes, through the valves, the bends, the cocks, the gauges, the filters, the sensors, up and out into the pipes! Those strong, gleaming pipes, stretched out across the ocean, mile after mile. Deep beneath the stormy waves, deep beneath the tempestuous clouds, lying flat on the rocky sea bed, surrounded by strange and ancient fish, by swirling weed and warty crustacians, by curious dogfish and the occasional shark, which nibbles at an oily rag caught on one of the securing pegs. But the gas rushes on, over caverns filled with blind, anaemic squids, over mountains taller than the Alps, through brightly coloured plants, shoals of scate and cod, along side rotting wrecks and discarded metal boxes. And the sea above tosses and turns and the gulls wail and women wonder if their menfolk on the ocean will ever return, as the gas silently passes on beneath, rushing through its walls of steel, welded perfectly every sixty feet. Then the gentle slope as the pipe rises out of the water and flows smoothly, beautifully, into that vast complex of modern technology, known as the gas works!

GASMAN. Of course I've had my times — I'm not saying it's all been bad, seen a sight or two as well. Well, I mean you're bound to aren't you, crawling around all them places. I remember one time, I was in this cellar, see, black as pitch it was, and me only with me standard issue torch, and that with the battery low. Anyway, I was looking behind this cupboard, right, real heavy thing it was, and I couldn't budge it. Now I was in a real hurry, seeing as it was the day of the match — Arsenal and United, and what a game that turned out to be! Three goals in the last fifteen minutes! If they'd kept the reserve off we'd been home and dry by half time — anyway, there I was heaving away at this cupboard, when suddenly, after a real big tug, the whole thing comes toppling down on top of me. Well, you can imagine my surprise, I wasn't going to stand in the way of *that* baby, so I neatly side step — a manouvre I picked up from Nijinsky I believe — and before I knows where I am, I'm staring down at a smashed open cupboard — split open like an over-ripe tangerine it did. Well, I'm not a squeamish man by nature, I've seen a thing or two in my time, but this really took the cake. . . .

JANET. Then just pipes! Nothing but pipes! Thousands and thousands of pipes! All different sizes and shapes and sorts. Pipes, pipes, pipes! Large pipes leading into smaller pipes, leading into smaller pipes, leading into large pipes! And taps and throttles and bends and curves, a maze of pipes and dials and gauges and dials. All filled cram full with gas! Then the biggest pipe of all shoots out of the tank and buries itself deep into the soil. Under fields and valleys it goes, under roads and lanes and motorways. Under streams and rivers, under woods and vales, under lakes and ponds and puddles, until suddenly it hits the town and is shattered into a thousand thousand tiny little pipes which weave in and out like the veins in an embryo. And just one of these teeny weeny little pipes makes its way up my garden path, under my door step, under my kitchen floor until it pops out in that cupboard, and hey presto, I can cook!

GASMAN. (*At same time as* JANET's *next speech.*) 'course I've come across some nutters in my time. Mad as hatters, some of them. Deny that they've ever had gas at all. Say that they're all electric — never had gas in the house! Deny it 'till they're blue in the face, they will, then make a pot of tea on the stove! Then of course there's the other type, the sort that comes out in a housecoat and slippers, and says "So you're the gasman! You can read my meter any time." One minute they're offering you tea and the next they're flashing their tits at you.

JANET. (*Same time as above.*) Do you realise how it feels to know all that has been done just so I can have this little flame? Those years and years of sweat and labour and bother, so I can sit warm here in my kitchen and cook meals for my beloved husband. It makes me proud to be a housewife — it makes me proud to be a woman! that's how it makes me feel. (*Pause.*) Did you say that you wanted to see my tits? Why of course, I mean it's not much to ask, is it, to see my mammary glands after all you men have done for me. It's small recompense, considering, wouldn't you say? (*Shows her breasts.*) There. What do you think of them? Not bad for a woman of my age, eh? Of course they're not as firm as they used to be, but none of us is getting any younger, eh? We all have to face a certain drooping of the flesh in the end. Please don't look so surprised, or I may ask to see your penis.

GASMAN. (*Standing.*) Really! (HARRY *enters.*)

HARRY. I can't find the damned thing anywhere . . What the hell's going on?

JANET. Oh, nothing much, I was just showing our gasman here my tits and he refuses to repay the compliment by showing me his prick — really most unreasonable of him. (*Pause.*)

HARRY. You'll have to excuse my wife — she gets upset at times. She's not her usual self today — time of the month, you know.

JANET. What did you say?

GASMAN. Oh, I quite understand, sir, no need to apologise.

JANET. You know, the first time with Harry he came in ten seconds!

HARRY. You know how it is — just a few days.

JANET. Ten seconds! No sooner than he was in there than, bang, it was all over! To be honest, I couldn't even be sure it *was* in there.

GASMAN. Of course, of course. The missus is the same.

JANET. That's right, that's right. It's all because my ovaries are contracting, ovums popping out, blood oozing down — that explains it all. You really will have to forgive me, but my vagina is full of my insides. Awfully sorry. Have to make allowances. I'm just a simple minded woman who's become bloody minded because of her period. I'm on the rag, having the curse, stuffed up with a vampire's pack lunch. Well that settles that. They're so unreliable — like clockwork, every month, all tears and sulks — far too moody. Have to handle her with kid gloves. Well fuck you, scum!

GASMAN. (*Pause.*) I've been thinking, sir, perhaps it's down here after all.

HARRY. Yes, perhaps you're right.

GASMAN. I think that cupboard looks a likely place, wouldn't you say?

HARRY. Yes, yes I suppose it does. And it has got a pipe running up to it.

JANET. Have you been listening? Have you been listening to one word I've said?

GASMAN. Well, in that case I think we should take a look, don't you?

HARRY. Good idea.

JANET. Hallo? Hallo? Can anybody hear me? Hallo, am I dead?

GASMAN. Let's see, it's a bit stiff. Here she comes — there, what do you say?

HARRY. Amasing — right under our noses.

GASMAN. That's how it is sometimes, sir. Now, let me see. 472 1417. There we are — all logged down, all ship shape and Bristol fashion!

JANET. Hallo God, is that you? This is me. I'm bleeding to death, dear Christ. But don't worry about me, I'll be all right. I expect Eve was just having her period — easy enough slip.

HARRY. And here are my shoes, right under the sink! Good lord, they're even polished!

GASMAN. Here we are, sir, all finished, until next time that is. Sorry to have kept you so long.

HARRY. No, no, not at all.

GASMAN. Well, I'll be off then.

HARRY. Let me see you to the gate.

GASMAN. That's very kind of you, sir. Goodbye, mam.

HARRY. Oh, and Janet, I shan't be home till late this evening, save the dinner, will you? (GASMAN *and* HARRY *exit.* JANET *stays still. Lights dim very slowly.*)

COSTUME PLOT: "PERIOD"

JANET: Street clothes
HARRY: Suit, without jacket
GASMAN: Overalls, green

PROPERTY PLOT

Two sets of knife, fork, spoon
Two bowls
Packet of All-Bran cereal
Jug of milk
Teapot, china
Salt and pepper pots
Dust pan and brush
Pair of shoes
Assorted china, in dresser
Two pieces of toast
Pack of teabags
Torch, (brought on by Gasman)
Notebook and pen, (brought on by Gasman)
Kettle

<u>SET DESIGN</u>   "Period"

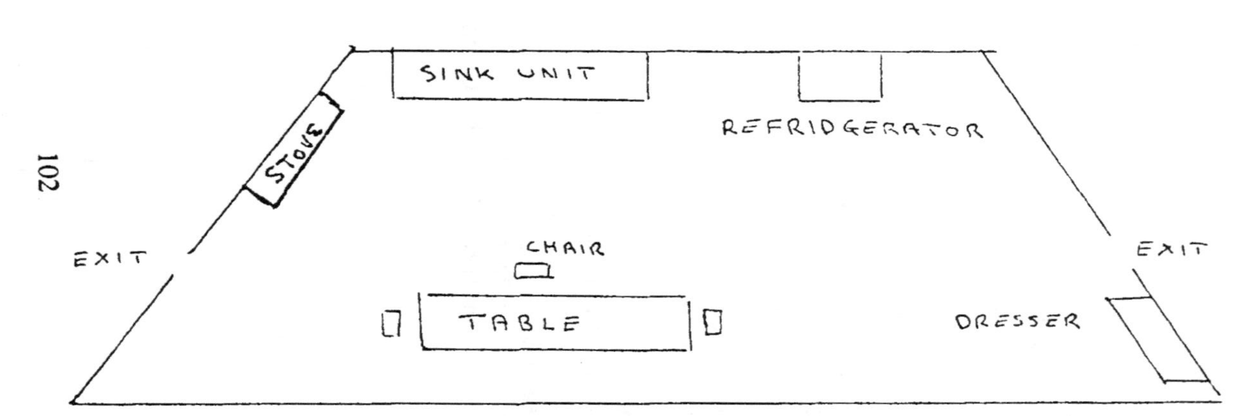

102

www.ingramcontent.com/pod-product-compliance
Lightning Source LLC
Chambersburg PA
CBHW070632120726
47909CB00004B/1400